Joseph Henry Shorthouse

Blanche, Lady Falaise

A Tale

Joseph Henry Shorthouse

Blanche, Lady Falaise
A Tale

ISBN/EAN: 9783337089283

Printed in Europe, USA, Canada, Australia, Japan

Cover: Foto ©Andreas Hilbeck / pixelio.de

More available books at **www.hansebooks.com**

BLANCHE, LADY FALAISE

A Tale

BY

J. H. SHORTHOUSE

AUTHOR OF

'JOHN INGLESANT,' 'SIR PERCIVAL,' 'THE COUNTESS EVE,' ETC.

London

MACMILLAN AND CO.

AND NEW YORK

1891

Et ait; Dominus de Sinai venit, et de Seir ortus est nobis; apparuit de Monte Pharan, et oum eo sanctorum millia. In dextera ejus ignea lex.

Liber Deuteronomii xxxiii. 2.
Vulgatæ Editionis.

ADVERTISEMENT

I FERVENTLY hope that I shall be believed
when I say, as I do most earnestly. that I have
in no case introduced any person with whom I
have been acquainted, either in Devonshire or
elsewhere, into this tale. I have called the
cathedral city Minsterley in order to mark
this fact. To the best of my belief no such
incidents as are here described ever took place
in Exeter. I have endeavoured to avoid the
use of names or titles which are in existence
at the present time in Devonshire. If I have
inadvertently erred in this regard, I hope that
the annoyance will not be great. I owe an
apology to the Premier-Viscount of England.

The only point upon which, I fear, I must

plead guilty, is in the case of some descriptive phrases about Devon, from which I have not been able to exclude all traces of affection and admiration for the people and the scenery of that delightful land.   J. H. S.

INTRODUCTION

I AM only a woman, and I am going to write this book in my own way, and I write it simply because I have been brought so near to all the actors of the story, and because it seems to me that there is something in their story which it may not be amiss for others to hear. If the human story be worth telling, it must be because the hearer receives from the telling something which he did not possess before. There is therefore in true art no such thing as realism, for it is just this quality of the hitherto ungrasped which is the ideal, and which alone gives to art any *raison d'être* at all.

I write this story, also, with other thoughts. The things which are seen are temporal, but the things which are unseen are eternal. The old world, with its form and guise, is rapidly passing away. A struggle for existence, for daily bread, such as the world has perhaps never seen, is close upon us, and before this struggle palaces and parks, statues and pictures, perchance, will be consumed, as they have been consumed before, in a *lex ignea*, a fiery law, but the eternal will survive; nay, it even seems to me that the very variableness and inconstancy of that which appears, are the means by which we see what the invariable and the constant are. The same types will return again. The Dux, the leader, will reappear. The Norman, the aristocrat, like my Lord Falaise, will come to the front. The oaks will grow again; Nature is more apt than any of us in recovering lost ground. The stars will fall from heaven, but by a baptism of fire, more terrible and searching than any that the world has known, new heavens and a new earth — and yet not so wholly new but that some recognition of the darling past will be possible — will reappear. Sin, the enemy, will triumph and will be slain — will triumph, for an error may be renounced yet its fatal sting remain; the consequences of one act of sin can never be revoked. What we see of Sin is its protean inconstancy; what is unseen is the dread result of an unchangeable law. If there be any lesson taught us by my story, it is the deceitfulness of Sin, and the piti-

less insistence with which it exacts its payment
to the full.   Nevertheless Sin will be slain, for
the Divine nature has known suffering, and the
inappeasable pang of unjust blame, and thus has
won for itself this supreme prerogative, that it
has achieved the revocation of an irrevocable
and appalling Past.   God Himself, who is also
the Son of man, has become the divine and
eternal redemption and rectification of all wrong,
since nothing but the Divine nature, which ab-
sorbs all things, and is all things, could rectify
the injury that has set all human relations
ajar.

In the meantime it may not seem useless to
record in a few simple pages how these truths
expressed themselves under the old feudal,
aristocratic, cultured life that is so rapidly
passing away.

My father was the son of a clergyman in
North Devon.   He was a wild irreclaimable boy.
He ran away from school, out of pure reckless-
ness, and engaged himself at a music warehouse
in London as an errand-boy.   Here he developed
an extraordinary aptitude for playing the violin.
He was taken notice of, and put in the way of
being taught, and finally became a professional

musician, wandering about the world after a reckless and unprincipled manner of life. He found in Paris a girl whom he married. She was a singer and *danseuse*, a Parisienne, and a benighted papist; but if there be another world where pure unselfishness is thought anything of, it will surprise me very much if it has not been said to my mother there that it was well done. She died when I was about twelve years old of the toil of bread-winning for husband and for child, and my father came back to London, bringing me with him.

I dread to think of the years that followed. The story of those wretched hours has nothing to do with the narrative which I have undertaken to relate. I did what I could, when I was old enough, by giving lessons in the French language and in music. I played both the piano and violin, but unfortunately I had no voice. At last, after some ten or twelve years, my father died. Then, when I was wondering what it would be best or possible for me to do, I received a letter from an aunt, my father's only sister, in Devonshire, who had frequently, out of her small means, assisted my father in his dire straits, inviting me to come and visit her. 'With your advantages of training and education,'—so she spoke in the innocence of her heart—'you might possibly find some employment for your accomplishments among the neighbouring families of distinction.'

I shall never forget that afternoon. It was indeed the beginning of a new life, but it was not any consciousness or reflection of this kind that affected me then; it was the sensation of the moment that moved me, and that lives with me now. After crowded streets and tall houses, that shut out all sense of distance and of space, after noise and toil and restless sleeplessness, an amazing stillness and calm. After the whirr and jar of third-class railway travelling, with its stain of dust and sulphurous smoke, I found myself suddenly, about four o'clock of a marvellous September afternoon, landed upon the narrow wooden platform of a roadside station in North Devon. A surprising hush—as the train, after stopping for a minute or two, steamed on—was the first sensation that struck my sense. Then, as I stood for a moment or two upon the narrow platform, a sense of wonderfully pure air was drawn into my lungs and system, a rapt sense of delight that kept me absolutely still, and lost to all sense of aught beside. Then gradually there came to me a perception that I was standing

upon a wide hill-slope, under a limitless expanse
of delicate propitious sky, beneath a soft blue
heaven and the fleecy whiteness of drifting cloud;
and that all around me, up towards the moor
above, down into the endless reaches of dingle
and widening plain, were orchards, laden with
russet apples, and brown pastures, and rushing,
tumbling brooks.   It was with no easy transition
that I understood a porter who demanded in no
very gentle terms —

' Is that trunk yours, miss ? '

Humbly explaining to him, and giving him
threepence — a habit which I had contracted
from my father's example — he condescended to
inform me that there was a gig and a boy outside the station from Trefennick, which he supposed was intended for me, and shouldering my
trunk, he conducted me to the gig, and saw me
off, with as much politeness as if I had been a
countess.   I shall never forget that drive, but it
is not my story that I am telling but that of
another.   I said very little to the boy or he to
me, I was so lost in the beauty of the scene.

After a drive of a little less than an hour
we came up a wooded lane to a little village,
standing round a hilly green.   At the opening
of the village were one or two old-fashioned

red-brick houses, with gardens in front of them, rather superior in accommodation to the cottages beyond. Before one of these the gig stopped. A tall, very gentle-looking and refined old lady came down the narrow path between the fuchsias, hydrangeas, and veronicas, and welcomed me with great kindness. A little maid, very clean, and with an immaculate cap upon her youthful head, accompanied her, and assisted the boy to carry up my box.

A delicious sense of rest, of odorous flowers, of kindness and of peace, pervaded the place. A tiny bedroom, such delicate white dimity, quaint black slender washhand-stands and chairs, and a four-post bed, welcomed me. What a contrast from the slums of London life!

We had tea, such a tea!—pikelets, roasted apples, and Devonshire cream, with pale old china with the Bourbon sprig.

After tea my aunt suggested that, as the evening was perfectly fine, we should take a little walk up the village.

'I will show you our church,' she said; 'it is a very fine church.'

It most certainly was. It stood upon a rising mound in the centre of the village, with the thatched cottages straggling round in uneven lines. A wide churchyard and patches of common ground surrounded it. All around us, as we stood on these grassy mounds, lay the Devon landscape of field and forest, and above us the soft Devon evening sky. It was more like a cathedral than a parish church, though it stood in the midst of these few thatched cottages, and these Devonshire commons and lanes. Against the solemn evening sky it seemed a mystic fabric of whitish-gray, almost raised from the earth, so ethereal it looked, as we walked up the sloping churchyard path.

The door was open, for an old woman was very fortunately doing something inside, and we went in.

As we entered the church it seemed as though the immense nave, between white pillars and arches of early English work, was unoccupied save by a Norman font that stood in the centre; and on either side, up the wide aisles, the uneven pale pavement spread itself in open expanse, unencumbered by seat or pew — a pavement of no common sort, but formed of such stones as only centuries can produce; gravestones scrawled all over with the names for which the West country is renowned — Pollexfen, Trevannion, Pomeray, Ralegh, Hawker,—

names which, overflowing from the ranks of the landed gentry, are found on the stones and floor-ways everywhere beneath your feet.

But for some two-thirds of this white extent of nave towards an exquisite screen of oak, with faint gold tracery and worn and broken figures, that caught the eye at once on entering the church, were oaken benches of three centuries' date carved at the ends with Scripture emblems. Beyond the screen a chancel and side aisles stretched themselves dimly ; all was white and unadorned save for the carved monumental stones on the walls and pillars, and the names of the dead beneath our feet, and for a strange fantasy of colour that came from fragments of ancient glass, coat armour, and broken forms of saint and warrior, that remained in the upper panes of the white windows.

Over all there seemed to breathe a waft of pure air from orchard and field, pure as from the untainted world of Paradise, to tell us of the unseen union between the church of the living and of the dead, between pure life and the struggle of the world which is miscalled life. I have felt in other old churches since, but I do not know that I ever felt before that day, a sense of the oneness of holy, if vague, emotion with that instinctive and unpremeditated art which is the mere result and reflex of ages of human life.

We went up the nave between the open seats, and my aunt showed me the seat where she sat, just in front of the curious and elaborately carved pulpit. Then we turned into the south chapel, another wide expanse of paved stone, surrounded by high windows of plain glass, and a profusion of crowded tablets on the walls. Between the chapel and the chancel were two altar tombs, with effigies of knights and ladies lying side by side, and upon these, and upon the tablets on the walls, and over the rough and uneven pavement, from fragments of brasses, and from the almost illegible inscriptions upon the stones, there was distinguishable in impressive iteration the name Falaise. Down the south wall beneath the high leaded windows, in which there was more than usual of the antique heraldic glass, was a long seat or pew of elaborately carved ancient oak.

'This is the Falaise chapel,' said my aunt to me, with a certain solemnity in her tone; 'they are the great people here.'

We sat down for a few moments in the long oak pew, looking across the knightly figures to the wide chancel, beyond which, beneath the high east window of white glass, a perfectly plain table of oak, evidently of great antiquity, served for altar. The clergyman, I learnt afterwards, was very old. After his day it was expected many changes would befall.

'You know,' my aunt went on, when we had sat for a moment silent, 'that it is said that they are Normans, that the patent of their title runs, "Viscount Falaise of Falaise, in the King's province of Normandy," and that it dates from the Conquest. You will see them on Sunday. They are staying at Trefennick; indeed, they stay a great deal here. Lady Falaise is very beautiful. Hers is what they call, I suppose, a romantic story. She was the daughter of a clergyman not far from here, on the north coast. He was an Oxford man. Lord Falaise, when a boy, came to read with him. He fell in love, as was natural, with this beautiful girl; but she despised him, I suppose as being a boy, and would not listen to his suit. Then there came down into the neighbourhood for a holiday rest a young clergyman — a very handsome and attractive, and a very clever man, a popular preacher. He preached in the churches about here. He took everybody by storm. He and

Blanche Boteraux — that was Lady Falaise's name — were very much together. They were engaged for two or three years. She gave herself wholly and utterly to him, and to his work in the great towns. Then he behaved very badly. She was supposed to have no money, though it afterwards turned out that she came in for a great deal. He broke off the engagement and married the daughter of an earl, with a great deal of money; "to help him in his work," he said.

'Every one said that it would kill Blanche Boteraux. It did kill her father. Then Lord Falaise — you will see him on Sunday — came forward again. She married him; but from what I hear and see, I fear that she is not happy. I suppose it was too late. They have been married twelve years, and have two beautiful boys.'

'I have an idea,' continued my aunt after a pause, 'that Lady Falaise may possibly be glad to engage you to take some part in the education of her boys. Lord Falaise has some peculiar notions about the education of boys. He does not approve of sending them to public schools, at least at a very early age. He also wishes them to be highly cultured. I should not be surprised if Lady Falaise would be glad for you to teach her boys French and the violin.'

Before I had been twenty-four hours at Trefennick I discovered something of which I had previously been utterly ignorant, which was that my aunt was very much respected by the county-people of the neighbourhood. On the afternoon of the first day after my arrival a very stylish carriage, with two servants, stopped in the little village road before my aunt's garden-gate, and some great lady of title, whose name I have forgotten, spent half an hour with her. I may say here that I was much struck, first and last, with my aunt's manner in her intercourse with these great people. She seemed to know all about them, and asked questions which were evidently very well received concerning their relations and connections, as to whom it was proper to inquire, but she never made the smallest pretension of belonging to their caste, nor did she ever speak of them, even when alone with me, in any other way than that in which you speak of people of whose existence you are acquainted with only through the newspapers. I afterwards learned, for I really knew very little about my aunt, that after her father's death she had been companion to a great lady in the neighbourhood, who was devotedly attached to her, and who left her a comfortable little income at her death. I mention these things because they seem to me to account for some things that occurred afterwards which otherwise might seem strange.

Curiosity, I confess, was at least as dominant in my mind as devotion, as I went to church on the first Sunday that I spent at Trefennick. It was a beautiful autumn day.

From the oak-carved seat in which we were, in front of the pulpit, we could see the long ornamented stall of Charles the First's time in the chancel from end to end. The Falaises came in just before the service began, from a small door that opened into the chapel straight from the grassy mounds without.

I have been wondering how it would be possible to describe Lord Falaise, so as to convey to those who read this story any idea of how he seemed to me; but I have not been able to satisfy myself, for I mix up so much of what I saw and felt afterwards with that first sight.

He sat farthest from me in the long pew, yet

I seemed to see him sooner than I did Lady Falaise.

He was one of those men whose contour and colouring give you the impression that you are looking at a picture — not that you have any sense of unreality, for, before some portraits of Gainsborough, the ordinary men you meet outside your gates wither up, not into unreality, but into nothingness; but there was an indescribable distinction and refinement about his appearance which made you think that you were looking at a portrait conceived and executed by some great master of the art.

He was a decidedly handsome man, somewhat above the middle height, of a fair complexion and auburn colouring; but, I think — and I have watched his face so often and under such different circumstances, and have studied portraits of him by the first artists — that the great charm of his face lay in his eyes. They resembled agates, being marked with distinct differences of tracing and shade, and had an expression of rest and distinction which made his face the most unusual I had ever seen. They were fringed with long soft eyelashes, which, however, seemed rather to increase than diminish the effect of reserved intentness which they produced. I am so exceedingly dissatisfied with this effort at description that I would rather not attempt to describe Lady Falaise, who sat nearest to me, with the two boys between her and her husband, at present. It will be sufficient to say that she looked to me like a beautiful princess, but very pale and sad.

The service was very plain. A choir of men and boys, who sat all together in front of the organ on the other side of the chancel, sang the canticles and hymns. The few worshippers were almost lost in the old open benches, which seemed themselves a mere speck in the centre nave of the vast church. An oaken roof, with carved angels, loomed above us, mysterious in sunny, dusty light; and in front was the mouldering rood screen, with its faded gilding and worm-eaten tracery, and the stately eastern window, beyond the white glass of which light fleecy clouds sped rapidly across the sky, driven by the fresh morning breeze, beneath a chequer work of varied tinctures of coat armour in the rich ancient glass of the upper panes.

I believe that my aunt wrote to Lady Falaise —at any rate she told me, a morning or two afterwards, that we were to go to the Court. On the way she entertained me with many traditions and stories of the neighbourhood, of which she had an endless store. In the church-yard she showed me a tombstone with the inscription—

Orate pro anima Radulph Node

the sepulchre, as the story ran, of a man who pretended to fly from the top of the tower, and broke his neck—a story concocted probably by the country-people from the name upon the tombstone, which they pronounced 'Noddy.'

Inside the park gates, wrought with iron scroll-work, the path lay beneath a slope of woodland beneath the moor, past oaks said to be a thousand years old, and commanded a view towards the south, limitless as it seemed, across the breadth of Devon, of countless shades and tints of woodland, now mellow and now gay, which went far to satisfy the longing heart with the perfection of their beauty and their shaded restfulness, till I could have fancied that here at last was 'Paradise regained,' the primal garden between the four great rivers rediscovered, but for the never-dying consciousness which is born with some of us at least, whose childhood has been sad, that Nature is only the half of life, and that through her most persuasive and beguiling

paths there wanders ever, bent on its destructive
and fatal work, a restless, stubborn, inappeasable
human will.

Across the faint undertones of such musings
I scarcely heard my aunt's gentle talk of how
perfectly the family were Norman, of the great
tithes of Trefennick paid to the abbot of Falaise
till the Reformation, and of the long line of
descent beyond the Conquest from the dim Car-
lovingian time.

I had never seen such gardens as those at
Trefennick before, and I have not often seen
such since. They were formed in terraces beneath the woods, dropping down into the valley
and the park. Beyond the wide lawns, fringed
with flower-beds, rich with autumn colour, stone
balustrades and broad steps divided terrace from
terrace, and from these mossy walks and paved
stairways you caught gracious and sunny
glimpses of the distant world of forest and of
plain.

The upper walk of these magic gardens was
a natural grassy terrace made perfectly straight
by the balustered wall, and bordered on the left
by the woodland, and on the right, towards the
valley, by a line of yew trees, of immemorial
antiquity, planted close to the parapet of the

terrace wall. On the side of the gardens canariensis and clematis, growing up the terrace wall, had climbed into, and flung themselves over, these dark, stern, ancient trees. Seen from the lower terrace, with their blazonry of purple and of gold against the sombre wall of yews, they seemed like the fairy life of a day coquetting with Eternity; but, on the farther side of the dark hedge, what with the shadowy wood on one hand and the sombre yews on the other, and the long vista stretching into the unseen distance, the walk always seemed to me weird and ghostly.

I am describing all this, as I knew it so well afterwards, for of course I did not see it all that morning as we walked up the drive to the Court.

Trefennick had escaped the mania for rebuilding, in the last century, which destroyed many a noble pile. Either the Falaises had not been sufficiently wealthy, or they had preferred to make what improvements they did make upon the old lines, for the house was built of small red brick, round a courtyard, with buildings of varying heights, and, but for the clusters and rows of Jacobean chimneys, would have had a somewhat castellated appearance. Some part of it was said, upon doubtful authority, to have been designed by the architect who built Hampton Court in the reign of Henry VIII., and many parts were overgrown with small ivy and ampelopsis, and virginia creeper, and wistaria, so that the whole had a mellow and venerable appearance, though I believe much of it, as it stands now, dates only from the beginning of the century.

We were shown through several rooms, every one of them a dream and vision of art, a recollection of past history, an epitome of human life. Every great house is this.

At last we reached a large and lofty room called the saloon, evidently from the French *salon*, a great parlour, furnished in silk and gold, with ivory and ebony cabinets, and great landscapes by Hobbima, Ruysdael, and Cuyp, and overlooking through three tall windows the woodland sweep of Exmoor, and farther off, beyond the misty lines of moorland, a long dark ridge, a slight blue thread along the horizon, hiding in its faint outline all the wild savagery of the tors and valleys of Dartmoor.

Above this view of earth, glorious and wonderful in itself, was another more wonderful and glorious still, for over the whole sky, which, through these high windows, seemed to absorb

and dominate the earth, from the distant horizon to the zenith above our heads, was spread
another world of cloudland and of heaven, of
blue sky, streaked with woof and texture of
riven cloud, delicate and suggestive as with
the handwriting of God; and again, in the distance, over the savage moorlands, rainstorms
and thunderclouds, startling in their contrast
with the serene heaven overhead. I saw this
marvellous sight then, as I stood at the lofty
windows, waiting for Lady Falaise, across the
pleasure parks of the rich; but I have seen it,
a message sent of God, over the back alleys of
foul cities — if only I had been more willing
to see.

In this room, flooded with the morning light,
with this perfect art within, and this wealth of
beauty and of teaching lavished upon us from
without, I saw and heard speak for the first
time her to whom I afterwards became so
passionately attached — Blanche. Lady Falaise.

She came from her boudoir. and I can fancy
it all so well. She had been working. but the
work had been laid aside. She had been reading, but the book had fallen at her feet. I see
her now, as she came into the room, as I have
so often seen her since.

Those who have loved will tell me how futile words are to describe the loved. A most beautiful woman — what paltry words are these! — stately and queenlike it is true, but so winning and attractive that such words seem false and libellous. Her features were boldly cut, yet not too large, and were faultlessly moulded, especially the nose and mouth; the latter being exquisite in its perfect lines. She never smiled, but now and again the lips seemed to form themselves, as to a fruitless effort and a forgotten art, with a result that sent thrilling through the fancy what a smile from her must have been. She had masses of light hair wreathed and piled over her head.

She received us with extreme kindness, and her manner was simplicity itself.

'Lord Falaise,' she said, 'had been extremely pleased with the idea that the boys should have the benefit of Miss Wand's instruction. Lord Falaise was unfortunately obliged to attend Petty Sessions that morning, or he would have been present to welcome us. Lord Falaise had somewhat singular views as regarded the education of boys — inherited, as she believed, from his guardian, and from some of his ancestry. He had sent them to a preparatory school for a year, for he considered it was well that they should be acquainted with life — indeed with all things — early, but he had taken them away at the end of the year, and he did not approve of sending them to a public school too soon. People said,' she went on, 'that public schools knocked the nonsense out of a boy, but Lord Falaise said that it was exactly the nonsense that he wanted to keep in.'

It was here, in a sudden pause, that one of those dreams of a forgotten smile formed itself for a moment upon the speaker's lips.

'If Miss Wand would talk French to the boys, and give them lessons on the violin — she had not the slightest idea whether they had any aptitude that way — Lord Falaise would be very pleased.'

It was very strange, almost terrible, to see how she never spoke of the boys as her own, or as though she had any right or wish respecting them. It was always what Lord Falaise said — what would please him.

'Miss Wand would like to walk through the rooms,' she said. I thought that she welcomed the change of occupation herself.

We went through many stately rooms, with doorways and window-frames painted with flowers and figures by Italian artists dead a century ago; the walls hung with portraits and with wide landscapes by Berghem and by Claude. Before some of these portraits Lady Falaise paused and told me something which she thought would interest me.

She stopped before one picture, the portrait of a young man in an Elizabethan dress: 'That is called the fatal picture,' she said. 'The young man whom it represents was killed in a tavern broil in London. An hour before the blow was struck, here in the wilds of Devon, this picture fell from its place, and, striking something in its fall, made a rent in the face just under the eye, precisely in the place, and of the size of the dagger-wound which caused the young man's death. You can see where the canvas has been sewn up.'

'It is a singular story,' I said.

'It is probably not true,' said Lady Falaise.

Then she suddenly flushed all over and said: 'I should not have said that; Lord Falaise believes it.'

At last we reached the great drawing-room, which occupied the side of the quadrangle opposite to the entrance and facing the east. It was an immense room furnished and decorated in white and gold, and somewhat sparsely hung with life-sized portraits. The sun had ceased to shine into it, never to return for the whole of the day. A gigantic chandelier of glass, containing, it would seem, a myriad lights, hung from the centre of the ceiling. The six great windows looked out upon a wide, square grass plot, and beyond, as far as eye could reach, down the solemn, weird, yew walk on the upper terrace—a walk made as it seemed for the pacing up and down of beings not of this world. The sun was shining brightly upon the landscape without, but even in the sunlight the outside view was a solemn and melancholy one, while in the cold and stately room itself, with the cordon of courtly silent figures standing in never-changing posture and rank, I felt such a heart-chill as I had never felt in any room beside.

Lady Falaise stood for some seconds looking out of one of the high narrow windows, then she turned to us with something like a shudder.

'I never sit here,' she said, 'alone. The saloon even, without the morning sun, is so much more cheerful, with its open view of the country and the sky. There is something terrible in these formal gardens and walks — something ghostly, as if, through them, the dead, the lost, the estranged, might be expected to approach.'

'If there be such a thing,' I said to my aunt,
as we came down the steps of the hall door, and
walked down the long drive, — 'if there be such
a thing as a broken heart, it is here.'

'She was a magnificent girl,' said my aunt, —
'a princess among young women. The man must
have had a heart of stone who deceived and
deserted her.'

'Not a heart of stone, aunt,' I said; 'no heart
at all in the sense you mean.'

PART I

I

Human life has often been compared to a tale, most frequently to a badly-written tale, but I do not remember to have seen a comparison between youth and the first chapters of a tale, as they come into the author's mind, and yet I seem to see a very close, nay, a startling analogy between the two. In the opening chapters, as the author sits down to write them, the *dramatis personæ* are unformed — they do not know themselves, they do not know their parts. Afterwards, when they have grown to full estate, when their characters and their persons are formed, their passions developed, their tendencies known both to themselves and to others, the tale goes swimmingly on; they act for themselves. The author cannot alter events, even if he wished to do so; he has only to record. Surely it is so in opening life. These young creatures come from an infinite unknown. Whither they are going they know not. They find themselves in a strange place; more than this, themselves they do not know; what they are, and what they will be, what resolves and what possibilities are theirs, they cannot know, for these things do not yet exist. Those around them, like the stupid author of the unmeaning tale, for the most part, so far from being helps and guides, are hindrances and stumbling-blocks, — *ignes fatui*, that mislead and cause these little ones to offend. It was said once that for a great mill-stone to be tied about the neck of such, and for themselves to be drowned in the sea of seas, were a happier fate; yet, when we come to think of it, this seems somewhat hard, for they themselves were nothing but the result of the same endless revolutions of Fate's wheel. To them, as to those to whom they were a fatal snare, had the same thing happened; and so, through the fleeting but unending years, this badly-told tale is repeated; and, except where a divine genius walks the earth, and the prompting of a divine spirit is felt, the same old tale is written and rewritten with the same dull, unwearying pen, the great story-weaver never seeming to tire of the worn-out plot; and youth and promise and hope, treading always in each other's footmarks, crowd the opening chapters of life's story, and darken them with the tedious fore-shadowing of coming woe.

———

The Reverend Doctor Boteraux was an Oxford Don of a decidedly antique type. He was very highly connected, being the younger son of a younger son. Till he was past fifty he had lived entirely in Oxford—in the Oxford of the old school, in that Oxford in which it was a principle of the Presidents of John's that there should be no houses between their college and the country.

He was a man of commanding appearance, and of suave and courteous manners. He was a very great talker, gifted with an inexhaustible flow of anecdote and epigram. When he was past forty years of age he surprised his friends very much by returning from the Continent engaged to a lady whom he had met in Switzerland. She was returning from India, where she had been devoting herself to Zenana work. She was, I believe, a very beautiful and superior woman, but whatever she was, she only lived a few years after her marriage, and died, leaving behind her a little girl. This second shock —

for his marriage must have been a very considerable shock to a man of his habits — succeeded
in finally uprooting Dr. Boteraux. He accepted
a college-living in the north of Devon, and
removed there at fifty years of age with his
young daughter.

Clyston St. Fay is a village not very far from
the coast. It lies in a hollow of the low hills,
buried entirely in orchards. The place is devoted to the apple. In the spring-time, when
you open your lattice in the morning, and see
the blue sky overhead, the pink and white blos-
soms throng and crowd about you, as if in welcome and in sympathy of enjoyment with the
joyous hour. Apples were piled in the autumn
on the oaken floors and landings of the houses,
above the wooden staircases, and in lofts and
garrets, and even on the uneven planks of the
living rooms. A strange penetrating scent of
apples filled the houses and the village and the
air.

From the earliest dawn of spring to the
latest autumn day nothing but apples seemed to
exist in this place. The very trees themselves
assumed a personality which seemed greater
than that of any human inhabitant. In sudden
drops and dingles of the orchards grew ancient

patriarchs, well known and revered from old time by generations of men. Vast, gnarled, twisted, moss-grown, they were spoken of as living, venerated, beneficent entities. Their death, when such a terrible event occurred, was mourned as a public calamity. Their illness was watched over by experts, and relieved by expedients handed down from the wisdom of ancient days. Side by side with such intense and valued existence, what was the life or death of a mere Devon lad, who could be replaced, by the score, from the farms or cottages around?

In the dip of this scented and secluded valley was an astonishing little church, roofed with moss-grown tiles, and boasting a Norman tower. It was a real church. It possessed a nave opening into side aisles with Norman arches, a votary chapel, and a chancel, with an oak communion table three centuries old. Its walls were covered with quaint memorial tablets, of a renaissance type, chiefly in memory of dead rectors. It had a richly carved pulpit of oak which rose so suddenly above and out of the high-backed pews, that the congregation might truly be said to 'sit under' the preacher, who dominated the little family groups, each in its own cherished domain, beneath him.

At the top of the village slope, that stood out green and fresh and sparkling in dew against the sky, just where the orchards began to give place to the oaks, to the left of the steep road that toiled upwards to the moorlands, were a pair of iron gates, with stone pillars crowned with carved acorns or fir-cones, which led into a courtyard, at the back of which the rectory stood.

It was altogether out of proportion to the size and importance of the village and the church, but no one who knows anything of the Devonshire livings, or of this one in particular, will be surprised at this.

Clyston St. Fay was entered in the King's Books as producing a certain annual income, but practically speaking nothing was derived from it. The living had always been occupied by men of wealth, who looked upon it as a favourite retreat when tired of Oxford life. It had one very great advantage — it was absolutely 'uninfested' with dissent. When the Rector walked down the stony precipitous village street between the cottages and the gardens (the cottage gardens were marvellous at Clyston St. Fay, especially in the autumn, with asters and gladiolas, and pampas grass and belladonna lilies and veronicas), on a showery, sweet-scented afternoon — the afternoons were mostly showery at Clyston St. Fay, with the western gale blowing over the moorlands from the sea-coast and the Atlantic — he was, allowing for the limited number of his subjects, about as great a man as could be found in Europe. Dr. Boteraux had brought down his college butler with him. He had brought a quantity of old English marquetry furniture, inherited from his ancestors, and of old china, old pictures, old books, and old wine, purchased by himself.

The people were proud of their Rector. They were proud of his appearance; they were proud of his butler, who immediately seized upon the most presentable lad in the village and speedily transformed him into a distinguished-looking footman, the admiration and envy of every village youth — but they were especially proud of his sermons.

Dr. Boteraux preached very short sermons, never exceeding twenty minutes in delivery, on the moral virtues, obedience to parents, duties to children, responsibilities of married people, and the like. They were admirably written, in a terse, simple, yet perfectly scholarly style, with a shrewd observance of human life, and a humorous appreciation of its eccentricities. in which the unlettered villagers recognised a common humanity as unerringly as a more cultured audience might have done. The sermons were based, of course, upon Scriptural characters, but the Doctor was singularly happy in the introduction of classic story, the vital humanism of which he portrayed with an instinct which came very little short of poetic art, making religion, what it might seem it was meant to be, the sustenance and not the scarecrow of human life.

As the moral virtues, though difficult in practice, are, fortunately for frail humanity, limited in number, the theme was soon exhausted; but the Rector was far too wise to lessen the effect by rewriting his sermons with diminished force. He preached them repeatedly, not at stated intervals, but varying their recurrence with a pleasing uncertainty. It was this repetition, apparently, that secured their popularity. The congregation of Clyston St. Fay recognised these admired productions with gratified familiarity, like the service itself. There was one sermon 'On Ingratitude to Parents,' drawn from the story of Absalom, which was an especial favourite. When, after the text was given out, the familiar words 'I might entitle this discourse "Absalom, or the Ungrateful Son,"' were heard,

it was delightful to see the entire congregation
settle itself down to enjoyment, as one may
see people settle themselves at the opera at
the commencement of a favourite air; and the
time never came when the repetition of the
final passage following upon David's despair-
ing cry, and touching upon the sacrificial love
of parents, suggested in part, as it was, by
the *Iphigencia in Aulis*, did not bring the tears
into some eyes.

'I write about two sermons a year,' the Rector
would say to a confidential friend over a glass of
port, ' just to keep my hand in, but the people
are restless under them. They don't feel comfortable till they have heard them two or three
times. "What do you think of that sermon,
Wike?" I say to my churchwarden in the vestry;
" that was a new one" — by the way there was
a sheriff of Devon named Wike in Henry the
Fourth's time, and the memory of man goeth not
back to the time when there was not a Wike
churchwarden of Clyston St. Fay. " Yes, sir,"
he says, "I know that; very good, very good, but
you won't easily beat the old 'uns, sir." You
see,' the Rector would add, with a twinkle in his
eye, ' I am very heavily handicapped. I have
to compete with myself.'

It had always been understood in the village, probably on the authority of Binns, the college butler, that the Rector was a man of property; but latterly stories had been afloat, traceable no doubt to the same source, of investments which had gone wrong, and of a chancery suit, which might be regarded either as a mine of wealth, or as a constant and fatal drain, according to the temperament of the sympathetic inquirer. There was no doubt, according to Binns's admission to very particular friends such as Mr. Churchwarden Wike, that the Rector was at times short of money. I am very pleased, for the credit of human nature, to be able to record that this knowledge increased the affection and respect which his parishioners entertained for Dr. Boteraux. It brought his personality into more sympathetic relation and understanding. It gave additional point to some telling passages in his sermons. As he walked down the village street he was regarded with still greater respect and affection than ever; and many a melon, marrow, or basket of choice apples — Cornish gillyflowers probably — not to say a goose, found their way up to the rectory, with dutiful respects, which otherwise, perhaps, would not have gone there.

The Rector's only daughter had been sent to school at some distant Cathedral town, and had spent her vacations very frequently in travelling with friends on the Continent. During the last two years she had lived entirely abroad at a school at Neufchâtel. During these years the Rector, partly it was supposed for the sake of income and partly for companionship, had from time to time received young men of family and fortune to read with him, either in vacation time or before going up to the university. These young men came and went singly or in couples, without creating much excitement at Clyston St. Fay, and the villagers had almost forgotten the existence of the Rector's daughter, when one Sunday morning. after a considerable interval of young men, they were suddenly startled by the appearance in the high, narrow box lined with green baize. beneath the pulpit, which was known as the Rector's pew, of a young girl dressed in white, with a black hat with ostrich feathers, and of striking and distinguished beauty. The villagers had not seen Blanche Boteraux since she was a little girl, but they had not the least doubt that this haughty young beauty was she. Her father had brought her into the church and deposited her in the pew some time before the service began.

Even the Rector's sermon was not listened to that day with the usual attention. It is to be feared that many of the congregation would have failed in an examination as to which of the moral virtues was dealt with that morning.

Blanche Boteraux did not make her way speedily, if indeed at all, at Clyston St. Fay, and it did not seem that she wished to do so. It was evident that she was shy and reserved, but the villagers asserted that she was disdainful and discontented also. But there was no disputing that she was a most beautiful girl. She had a lofty, searching look in her brown eyes, as though she were seeking for something which she never found, that disconcerted those whom she met in the village lanes, and prevented any familiarity or freedom of intercourse. Some of the simple people went so far as to doubt if she were perfectly sane.

'Mad with pride, I call her,' said Mrs. Wike, the churchwarden's wife; 'nothing is good enough for her. I believe she despises her own father. I watched her during the Absalom sermon on Sunday week.'

But Mrs. Churchwarden Wike was wrong. Blanche Boteraux was not mad, at any rate not at that time; she was only suffering from that most commonplace of complaints — the inability to reconcile a lofty ideal with the tedious surroundings of everyday life. Inheriting from her mother a passionate, sacrificial spirit, and from her father her beauty of form, and a certain sympathy with aristocratic instincts, of which last tendency she was probably unconscious, though it made her walk more difficult through the world's low places, and having, in her school-days, and especially during her residence at Neufchâtel, imbibed the boldest aspirations of Christian Socialism, the petty needs and incidents of village life, and the formal maxims of an antique theology, appeared to her infinitely poor and mean. She failed to grasp the link, if there be such an one, that unites the daily action, the little paltry deed, with the vast result of perfect redemption and salvation of the race. She might be thought of as perpetually waiting for the injunction of the Prophet to do some great thing; consequently she did nothing, and, doing nothing, and uprooted from familiar and congenial soil, she was unhappy.

She had not been in the village, however, much more than three months, when another excitement befell the quiet place. It was reported, doubtless from the information of Mr. Binns, that a very distinguished young man — in fact a lord — was coming down to read with the Rector between his leaving Eton and going to Oxford. There had been some difficulty, Mr. Binns believed, owing to Miss Boteraux's being at home; but this young lord was the ward of a duke, a very old and especial friend of the Rector's, and his father had been a college pupil, so that all difficulties had been smoothed over. His horses had already been sent down, and he himself was expected every day. The excitement in the village was very great.

I am in possession of a copy of the letter which the Duke of Chester and St. Clare wrote to his old college friend, Dr. Boteraux, on this occasion, and I have been very much exercised in my mind whether I ought to reveal it to the public or not. It is so genuinely private; it treats upon such very solemn and important subjects relating to the highest classes, that I have long hesitated before finally determining to print it here. It runs thus —

THE PRIORY,
HAWKRIDGE ST. MARY,
GLOUCESTERSHIRE, August 23, 18—.

MY DEAR BOTERAUX,

I write to you, as perhaps the oldest friend I have left, to ask a favour which I hope it may be in your power to grant. The son of poor Falaise, whom you will remember at St. Nod's — dear old St. Nod's — and who was connected with me by many ties, severed by his untimely death — his boy, who is a godson and a ward of mine, is leaving Eton and going to Oxford. You will remember Falaise, though he was so much younger than either of us. He left his son to my care, and I have done what I could for him. He has got through Eton pretty well. I rather like Eton. The boys have private rooms, and there are some remains of gentlemanly feeling about the place. But I hear that St. Nod's is much changed. Oxford is much changed. I was there a month ago, and was dining at the Vice-Chancellor's. A boy sat opposite to me, near to Lady Blank, the son of a Secretary of State, grandson of a Peer. Lady Blank said something to him which he did not hear. Instead of speaking properly, he said ' Whaart ? '

'Gad! young man,' I thought to myself, 'it's a fortunate thing for you that you were not my father's son. He would have caned you to within an inch of your life for that.'

Now I should like poor Falaise's boy to come to you for a month or two before going up to St. Nod's. Will you have him ?

Your daughter, I suppose, is still abroad. She must be quite a young woman by this time.

My dear Boteraux,

Yours ever,

CHESTER AND St. CLARE.

When Dr. Boteraux read this letter, he said to himself, 'I cannot refuse this boy. There may be some trouble about Blanche, but it is such an out-of-the-way place, and she can go and pay some visits.' So he wrote a letter to the Duke, saying that the boy might come for a year if he liked, and that he should want three hundred pounds.

The Duke received this letter as he was sitting with his secretary in the library of his favourite residence in Gloucestershire.

'And the amount will be right?' said the secretary.

'Oh, quite right,' said the Duke. 'I wish he had said five hundred.'

Then as the secretary moved into the adjoining bay of the library, where he did his work, the Duke called to him—

'Jones, Jones, ahem, make a mistake. Make it five hundred. I think I heard something of Boteraux being short of cash; and—Jones, don't put it to the trustee account. Put it down to mine. It's Falaise's boy,' he added in a lower tone, in apology to himself and to Mr. Jones.

BLANCHE BOTERAUX was sitting, on a fair autumn afternoon, in the little upstairs' room which she called her own, reading the *Journal Intime* of Henri-Frédéric Amiel, and looking out over the fading landscape to where the gathering night-clouds shadowed the distance, with those questioning, urgent eyes of hers. Whatever she had to complain of at Clyston St. Fay, she had at least this, and she felt it herself in her most discontented moods, the priceless gift of delicious silence — a gift which thousands of the tormented of this world never get, though they would give all they have for one hour of it. In the hush of the outside world a supreme thought, partly suggested by the book before her, partly the flash of her own spirit, but never destined to be perfectly realised in the light, was passing across her brain, when ——

'Please, Miss Blanche,' said the old housekeeper, who had nursed her as a child, opening the door, after knocking,—'please, Miss Blanche, Mr. Binns says that Lord Falaise is come, and he is in the drawing-room, and the Rector is out, and will you go down?'

The girl rose suddenly to her feet, her face flushed with annoyance. She stood for a moment looking at the old servant as though some terrible outburst was imminent, then, as it would seem, restraining herself by an effort, she passed the housekeeper without a word, and went down the shallow flights of the wide, many-turning oaken staircase.

The drawing-room at the Rectory was a large low room, with a wide bay window at the end, almost the width of the room, with many separate sashes with small panes of glass, the woodwork all painted white. This window looked out upon a park-like field, in which two or three tame deer were feeding—a reminiscence of the deer in the paddock at old St. Nod's. The Rector also reared pheasants in this field, which was very extensive. The drawing-room was crowded with marquetry furniture, and with old pictures and china, and strange Indian and foreign knick-knacks, gods and dragons, and carved ivory. The pictures, when the slightest

ray of light fell upon them, shone out suddenly
with a brilliancy and life which was little short
of miraculous; but the frames were old and
dingy, the window hangings were worn and
rotten, the curios and idols that were strewn
about with reckless profusion were dim, as with
the shadow of the faded years — the years that
had taken with them so many hopes and lives
and loves. Outside, the low western sun shining through the falling leaves, and the yellow
tints of autumn, made the woodland brilliant
with a subdued radiance, and through a mist of
rain seemed to perfect the magic vision of the
room; it became like the enchanted precinct of
a dream.

When Blanche Boteraux entered that faded
room, with the gone colours of its hangings,
and the fadeless beauty of the pictures, and
the strange, dreamy sense of past existence that
filled the place, she saw, I suppose, the most
beautiful boy then in England. There is a
portrait of him in crayons, as he was at that
time, in the great drawing-room at Trefennick,
by the celebrated artist Mr. Sands, and standing
before it and marvelling at its strange beauty, I
make this statement advisedly. To the perfect
symmetry of feature and of contour, as of a

Greek Antinous, was added the marvellous expression of the eyes, in which was united something of that consciousness of sacrifice which, according to story, the Greek Antinous knew, and something of an expression which no pagan ever had — the expression of an instinct which comes to the peoples of the Christian renaissance, the gift of a long heredity of inheritance in the memories, the struggles, the passions of a chivalrous past.

More than this, when Blanche came into the room, she saw this boy in the most beautiful setting that could easily be imagined. He had risen as she came in, and behind him, through the quaint white sashes of the bay window, were drawn the streaks of yellow woodland, and the sad mystic blue of the autumn sky, and amid the long wet grass stood the deer, drawing with wistful, timid glances close to the house; yet in spite of all this, she looked at this boy as though he were a toad.

'I am so sorry that I have disturbed you, Miss Boteraux,' he said, almost breathless with eagerness. 'I begged the servant not to tell you that I had come. I could have gone to my room, or anywhere, till Dr. Boteraux came in.'

She looked at him with her full, steady

glance, not searching, but absolutely indifferent and calm.

'Won't you sit down?' she said.

It was not a cheerful reception, but the instinct and pluck of his caste pulled him through.

'I am sure that I feel how very kind it is of Dr. Boteraux to take me,' he said. 'My god-father, the Duke of Chester, feels the obligation immensely. He wrote me quite a long letter — he did indeed — to impress upon me how grateful I ought to be to Dr. Boteraux. I hope I am.'

There was no answer at all to this, and there was a pause of some seconds. Then the boy began again —

'This is a most beautiful place. I think you must be very happy here.'

'Happiness does not consist in beautiful places,' she said.

If the grammatical construction of this sentence had been correct, which it was not, the meaning would still have been slightly obscure; at any rate, it was of too abstract a nature for George Falaise to grapple with, and he remained silent.

Presently, as the silence became embarrassing, he said —

'I never saw so many apples.'

As this was an undeniable and distinct drop from the tone of the previous remark, Blanche did not condescend to notice it. There was a longer pause than ever.

Then, with the air of a Christian girl of the second century being led to martyrdom, she rose from her seat and said—

'You would like to go round the garden.'

'Oh, I beg that you will not trouble yourself, Miss Boteraux,' he said desperately; 'I can go by myself. I can go to my room. I can do anything till Dr. Boteraux comes in. Besides, it is raining.'

'No,' she said, with that calm superiority of tone that prevents all discussion,—'no, we will go. It was only a shower. It always rains here.'

He followed her out meekly, through an old-fashioned side door, with a glass sash, on to a gravel path which led round the field-park for a circuit of over a mile. The rain had ceased. The path was bordered on either side by lofty trees; it was very narrow and uneven, at places dropping into dingles and now widening into copses and little woods, and more than once crossing running brooks by rustic wooden bridges. It was more beautiful in the spring-time, when the ground was covered with wild flowers, than in the autumn; but on this bright autumn afternoon, at least, the scene was impressive and soothing, with the thinned foliage letting in the blue sky and shining light, and the bright yellow rustling leaves scattered almost equally upon earth and bough and air. Both the boy and girl, in their different ways, felt something of the influence of the season and of the hour.

Immediately on leaving the house the path dropped away suddenly in the direction of the village, crossing a rustic bridge, and then climbing a steep ascent towards the upper part of the park.

As they stood on the bridge for a moment a lovely view of the narrow valley, opening upon the wide distant plain, lay before them, and exactly in front rose the tower of the village church.

This suggested another remark to the boy. He felt it his duty to make remarks.

'Have you nice people in the village?' he said.

'Oh, very nice!' she answered at once; 'I am astonished how nice they are, considering how shamefully they have been neglected.'

'I should not have thought that that could have been said in Dr. Boteraux's parish,' he said.

'Oh, my father!' she said, as though the idea was fresh to her. 'Yes. But my father is of the old school, and he is a college Don and not a parish priest. That is one of the anomalies of our Church system;' and she stood, in her white frock, upon the mossy plank bridge looking out, with her steadfast seeking gaze, across the distant Devon plain towards the southern sky, as if in search of a system or a church without anomalies.

'This is a most extraordinary girl,' thought George Falaise; 'but she is awfully stunning;' and in some sense or other I imagine that he was right.

As she did not say anything more, and still remained standing upon the bridge, he felt bound to make another observation.

'I wonder,' he said, 'why it is, when we look upon anything like this — woods, you know, and — what do you call it? — the distant plain, and the sky, — you, you think it is so beautiful. Why do you?'

Now it may seem a curious thing, but this remark attracted the girl more than, a moment or two ago, she could have supposed that any word of her companion could have done. It seemed to her Socratic.

She had read, over and over again, translations of one or two of Plato's dialogues, with a desperate determination to find out what it was that was so supremely great in them; and she had succeeded in grasping that peculiarity of Socrates,.which made him so great and so detested — the habit of asking questions which nobody could answer. She looked at her companion with a glance that so nearly approached to interest that it sent the blood dancing through every vein.

But in addition to this conception there was another which gave her a strange sort of pleasure; she felt that she had not the least idea of what answer it would be possible to make.

If only the foolish boy had had the sense to hold his tongue! but the garrulity of his caste overcame him.

He felt bound to relieve what he fancied was her embarrassment, not knowing, ignorant boy as he was, that at certain moments the female mind delights in being embarrassed.

'I suppose,' he said, — 'I suppose that if I knew more about tints, and gradations of light and shadow, and foregrounds, and all that sort of thing, I should understand it better.'

The mystic light, the unknown Infinite, faded from before her at these commonplace words.

'Perhaps you would,' she said; and, turning away with a relapse into her former cold distrait manner, she left the bridge.

They had not gone on very far up the ascent beyond, before she suggested that they should turn back. It was a very long way round the plantation, she said,—over two miles. Her father would probably have returned by this time.

She led George, by a lower path than the one that had brought them from the house, through a formal, old-fashioned garden, climbing the hill in neglected terraced walks and steps, and full of a wild untrimmed growth of perennial plants and flowers. At the foot of the terraced walls were lines of St. John's wort, with banks of hydrangeas behind them, and the terraces themselves were perfectly clothed with myrtle and yellow holly in closely clipped hedges against the walls. Above them, as they came up, was the stone façade of one wing of the rectory, containing the dining-room and library, built in the last century by a rector of more than usual opulence. The moulding of the windows and

the cornice along the top of the house were
richly carved in stone, mellow and moss-grown
in the soft moist Devon air of a hundred
summers. As they reached the upper terrace
the Rector appeared, coming from the house.

'My dear boy,' he exclaimed heartily, 'I am
delighted to see you. I am so sorry that I was
out. However, I see that my daughter has been
doing her best to entertain you, so I hope that
you have had nothing to complain of.'

Blanche Boteraux looked as if she was thinking that if her companion concurred in this
sentiment he was easily pleased.

'Come into my den,' said the Rector. 'I
want to look at you. I want to talk to you of
your father and of the Duke. Ah! you have
your father's eyes — the Falaise eyes — and
when did you see the Duke?'

'I have not seen my godfather, sir, for some
time,' replied the boy; 'but I have a letter
from him, in which he desires me to express
the great obligation he feels himself under to
Dr. Boteraux, — his oldest and his best friend,
he says.'

'Yes,' said the Rector more quietly; 'that
is like him — very like him. He always saw
others through the glow of his own nature.'

When the small party assembled at dinner, it was quite a stately meal. Mr. Binns was resplendent in his best Sunday suit, and the village lad, now a tall young man, for whom the village tailor had succeeded in making a footman's livery which would not have disgraced Plymouth, was on his best behaviour. Then both of them 'my lorded' George to their hearts' content if not to his. On the table were antique candelabra and side-dishes of silver, full of the late roses. Blanche wore a white silk dress very simply made, and a necklace of great pearls. The dress was one which she had worn on festal days at the Pension at Neufchâtel; the pearls she had found in the drawer of an old-fashioned bureau in her bedroom at Clyston St. Fay.

The Rector did most of the talking. Had there been any opportunity for his interposing, which there scarcely was, George was too much occupied with looking at his youthful hostess to avail himself of it. He had never been so happy in his short but not unhappy life. The constant stream of anecdote and epigram that flowed from Dr. Boteraux's lips formed a lively and agreeable accompaniment to the moderate but excellent meal of soup,

mutton, and game.   Blanche said nothing.
She ate very little, drank water only, and evidently regarded the repast as an inexcusable
waste of time.   She left the room at the earliest
possible moment.

The two men, if they might be so called,
remained a considerable time in the dining-
room.   When they came into the shadowy
drawing-room, dimly lit by shaded candles, they
were evidently on the best of terms.   Blanche
was seated at the piano, the only modern thing
in the room.   One of the duties which she
recognised was to play to her father at night.

I imagine that there are different styles of
music, or that, at least, some people call something music which others do not.   Formerly
there was something which was called music in
which musical tone occupied a not unimportant
place.   That style seems to be out of fashion.
I fear that Blanche Boteraux's musical education must have been neglected at Neufchâtel, for
she played a delicious melody which would have
been called flat by the admirers of concert pitch,
into which subdued euphony she threw a devotion of soul, and a whole nature, curbed and
suppressed during the day.   The wailing, seeking, passionate notes wandered through the mel-

low yet ringing keys questioning heaven and earth for an answer that never came.

George did not understand it, but he thought it the most wonderful thing that he had ever heard. Dr. Boteraux was perfectly quiet, not a single anecdote or epigram passed his lips. Blanche sang a little but did not seem to enjoy it.

·'I don't care for words,' she said.

The doctor kissed his daughter. Poor George! fancy, kissing this glorious creature.

'I think you play better every night,' he said; 'George and I will have a pipe and come to bed.'

THE next morning George Falaise took his Sophocles and found his way to a seat outside the drawing-room window. He had not sat there long, and had not read any Sophocles, when Blanche Boteraux came out of the house and came towards him, evidently with the intention of wishing him good morning. He was pleased with this; his limited experience of women not teaching him that it was the worst possible sign.

'Good morning, Lord Falaise,' she said.

'Oh, don't call me Lord Falaise,' he broke out, almost crying as he stood up; 'I can't bear it all day long. Call me nothing — unless,' he added suddenly, with a happy audacity, 'you would call me George. I wouldn't presume upon it; I wouldn't indeed.'

'Very well — George then — if you like it best,' she said. She did not say it, but her manner added as plainly as if spoken in words, 'You are only a boy.'

He felt very much suppressed—he had sense enough for that—but he rallied sufficiently to say—

'I did so enjoy your music last night. I never heard anything like it. I wonder how it is that some notes and sounds please us so much, and some not at all?'

This was something like his question of the day before, which had attracted her towards him for a moment; and she felt that it was, but it did not attract her to the same extent now.

She stood looking before her, with that fixed, steadfast look of hers, over the dewy grass and the faded woods.

But it was not the gardens and the faded woods and the soft Devon air that stirred him to the heart's depths, but the sight of this girl standing before him, despise him as she might.

'This is a beautiful place to wake up in,' he said.

'I should like to wake up in a place where there was something to do,' she said,—'I should like to wake up'—she grew more passionate as she went on—'in some back slum in the East of London; in some horrible court where the people are starving and needing help. Do you know the East of London?'

'No,' he said, 'not at all. I never was there in my life.'

'But there is an Eton Mission,' she said; 'did not you belong to that?'

'No,' he said; 'I fancy it's for fellows who have left——'

'Yes, yes,' she said honestly, 'no doubt. I don't suppose you could join while you were at school. But you will now?'

'I am going to Oxford.'

'But there is an Oxford Mission.'

'Is there?' he said blankly; 'I did not know that.'

'Yes, there is. And you must join and go up to the East End in the vacation; you will, won't you?'

'I had rather be here,' he said.

They had been sitting down during this colloquy, but now he rose and stood facing her, I rather think in self-defence. He felt a diminished ignominy in taking his lecture standing rather than sitting.

They were a striking pair, equal in beauty,

but otherwise strangely ill-assorted. She, with
a passionate yearning for what she thought
was self-denial, but which, as likely as not,
was but the outcome of a profound selfishness;
passionately refusing everything that other
people seemed to like; earnestly desiring, without thought of self so far as she knew self, to
follow in her mother's footsteps, to walk in
the teaching of that school in which she had
been brought up, to raise the poor, to succour
the needy, with the Divine aid to suffer and
to feel. He, aristocrat to the finger-tips,
kindly, good-natured, seeking always for the
pleasant thing to say; optimist to the backbone, as was natural in the offspring of a
race which had enjoyed all the good things of
life, so far as there were any good things, for
more than a thousand years; capable of sacrifice where, to speak vulgarly, the game seemed
to him worth the candle, otherwise not; modest
in the sense that he never thought of improving
anybody, always of raising himself; selfish in
this sense, and perhaps in others, but with a
selfishness that reacted upon those around him
to their infinite gain.

I have before me a diary written by Blanche
Boteraux in these days. I do not know whether

I shall be able to bring in many extracts from this diary in the future pages of this story. I should be very glad to do so; but a narrative of this kind is very difficult of accomplishment, and one never knows beforehand what the possibilities may be. I think, however, that I cannot do wrong if I insert here one or two extracts, which, from the date attached to the passages, evidently were written at this time.

' *October* 3. — I have been reading Amiel this morning, always with an inexpressible attraction; for what he says appeals to the heart — a man of such power and genius, yet so pitiful and help-less. As he says here —

'"I have never felt any assurance of genius, or any presentiment of glory or happiness. I have never seen myself in imagination great or famous, or even a husband, a father, an influential citizen. This must be taken as a sign. What dreams I have are all vague and indifferent. I ought not to live, for I am now scarcely capable of living. Recognise your place. Let the Living live. Accept the cup given to you with its honey and its gall. Bring God down into your heart. Make within you a Temple of the Holy Spirit. Be diligent in good works; make others happier and better."

'It must be true what Julia Genest used to say to me at Neufchâtel, that Amiel was more a woman than a man. These are a woman's words. This is the annunciation, which has shown to many a woman what she may become.'

'And again he says —

'"To be misunderstood even by those whom one loves is the cross and bitterness of life. It is the secret of that sad and melancholy smile on the lips of great men which so few understand; it is the cruelest trial reserved for self-devotion; it is what must oftenest have wrung the heart of the Son of Man; and, if God could suffer, it would be the wound we should be for ever inflicting upon Him. . . . Alas! alas! never to tire, never to grow cold; to be patient, sympathetic, tender; to hope always, like God; to love always!"

'These are a woman's words, not a man's.'

The next extract is evidently original, and I cannot help thinking has some reference to George Falaise.

'Men are so strange, even those of them with whom one feels it possible to live. They occupy willingly and of their own choice such a low standpoint. Provided the trivialities of life are decently met — what they call "form" — they have a supreme, I might say a superb, contentment, which is intolerable from its self-sufficiency, and, if I must say it, from its power. And I suppose that there are women even who — '

' And again, this time from Amiel —

' " Not a blade of grass but has a story to tell, not a
heart but has its romance, not a life which does not hide
a secret which is either its thorn or its spur.   Everywhere
grief, hope, comedy, tragedy, even under the petrifaction
of old age, as in the twisted forms of fossils, we may dis-
cover the agitations and tortures of youth.   This thought
is the magic wand of poets, and of romancists, and of
preachers; it strips the scales from our fleshly eyes, and
gives us a clear view into human life; it opens to the ear
a world of unknown melodies, and makes us understand
the thousand languages of nature.   Thwarted love makes
a man speak many tongues, and grief transforms him
into a diviner and a sorcerer."

' These, again, are the words of a woman, not
of a man.

' But are there women — how is any woman
to be equal to these things?   Henri-Frédéric
Amiel was not equal to them, and he called
himself a man !   But Lord Tennyson says —

' " Woman is not undeveloped man,
But diverse: could we make her as the man,
Sweet Love were slain. . . .
Yet in the long years liker must they grow; . . .
Till at the last she set herself to man,
Like perfect music unto noble words; . . .
Yoked in all excellence of noble end,
And so through those dark gates across the wild,
That no man knows."

'"Till at the last she set herself to man,
Like perfect music unto noble words."'

These two lines are written over again with extreme niceness and care.

A day or two afterwards she writes, evidently out of her own thought —

'There is an undertone, a minor key, running through all we do or think, if we could only hear it — a certain musical note, so attenuated that only in favoured moments of the soul can the finest ear perceive it, which would dominate all our passions and actions to a perfect harmony were it only heard and felt.'

It seems to have occurred to Dr. Boteraux, after George had been about a month at the rectory, that it would have been better for his daughter to pay a visit to some friends, and accordingly she was absent for about two months. I imagine that the interval appeared very dull to the two men who were left at Clyston St. Fay, in spite of the fascination of Sophocles, enlivened by excursions into Cicero and Juvenal.

Of course there was shooting for George Falaise, but I am told that there is satiety even in shooting partridges over a muddy field. He had his horses, it is true; but he had no one to ride with except the Rector, who rode very sedately, and whose fund of anecdote was by this time pretty much exhausted. Blanche makes no mention of this absence in her diary, which is full of such passages as I have quoted above, interspersed with extracts from books which she had been reading; but I fancy that on her return she felt some sort of pity for this lonely boy, so patient and so faultlessly polite.

It is not in female youthful human nature, however addicted to the study of Henri-Frédéric Amiel, and the amelioration of back slums, to resist altogether the silent pleading of respectful and devoted eyes. At any rate, when Blanche came back towards the end of January, she condescended to walk with George Falaise.

There is something singularly impressive about this time of year in Devon. Through the bare woods and over the desolate moors there wandered a persistent undertone that was sorrowful only in the sense that, without sorrow, the divine seriousness of life would be unknown. It was impossible for the most thoughtless not to feel something of the solemn lesson that the season taught.

Up the slopes of meadowland, where the dead grass afforded but a scant sustenance for the deer, which had to be fed by hand, through the drives and openings of the woods, by the lonely cottages of the woodmen and keepers, Blanche had wandered one morning, two or three days after her return, till they had reached the nearest point of the moor overlooking the great Devon plain. Here, where the oaks became stunted and twisted by the sweeping of the storm-wind from the sea, their upper branches white and sere, and covered with lichen, the two stood for some time looking at the scene, not because they were thinking much about it, but because there seemed nothing to say.

But what they saw was lovely enough to have kept any one at gaze. Overhead the day was bright and radiant, with a clear blue sky, such a day as now and again visits Devon — nay, other places also — in the severest winter, when it seems that summer returns to earth as if to bid it a last farewell, or to restore faith to men's minds. She finds indeed a changed scene to shine upon. In place of those fresh and green woods, those flowery fields, and the waving of tall and feathery grasses, this summer sun and azure sky, beautified, partly by contrast, partly by a mysterious and touching fitness, a world of departed colour and faded tints. Withered and bleached grass of a strange unearthly whiteness fringed the sloping banks and the summits of the fields; and, illumined by the brilliant sunlight, cast the delicate tracery of its empty seed-pods and fairy branches against the intense yet pallid blue, and deceived the eye with a soft-spreading halo or mist of whiteness stretching beyond and above itself, and gradually shading itself off into the delicate blue. A few surviving flowers of ragwort and hawkweed, withered by the winter frosts, remained of all the company of summer flowers, and in the place of these lost companions wreaths of haws and berries hung from the low hedges, and from the bare branches of the nut woods.

So much for the near foreground, but the distance revealed quite a different view. As these two young creatures stood upon the barren field, they looked over a great world-plain, inviting with mocking falsehood where to choose ; and whereas over their heads a cloudless heaven and serene sky stretched themselves, promising and hopeful, in the distance a dark canopy of gathering rain-clouds hung above a dark horizon, beneath which long rays and streaks of light shot across the far landscape, gilding the russet stretches of the bare oak woods, and breaking ever and again into a sudden flash and blaze, as the sunlight caught some tower or some village casement deep buried in the woodland.

They stood for some time in silence, apparently looking at this scene. Suddenly the boy spoke —

'Blanche,' he said; she knew that something startling was coming from the unusual address — 'Blanche, I want to ask whether you think that at any time — I don't mean of course now, but at any time — you think it might be possible that you might marry me?'

'No, George,' she said, without any hesitation, 'I don't.'

'Why?'

'It is not a fair question,' she said; 'but I will answer it, to you, because I think that you are a good boy. A woman should "set herself to man, as perfect music unto noble words." If ever I marry, it will be to such a man as this, and I do not think that you are he.'

It might seem at first sight that this sentence was incoherent, and the meaning anything but clear, but the boy seemed to understand it at once.

'No,' he said, almost laughing, but with a catch in his breath which spoke of something else than laughter, ' I should think not. Why I want to marry you is because you will raise me and do me good.'

' Ah! you are mistaken,' she said more softly; ' you will find some other girl.'

' Yes,' he said, with a contemptuous irony which was effective by its very unconsciousness, ' another girl!'

They came back down the steep path over the strewn and withered leaves. The rain-clouds were sweeping from the valley across the sun, and the bareness and chill of winter was on the woods and on the blackened grass. A blank depression and presentiment settled down upon Blanche's spirit. It seemed to her as if she were walking in a troubled nightmare, amid difficulties which were absurd, yet from which she was utterly unable to extricate herself. It seemed to her, at least for the moment, that in all the illimitable universe, limitless as the sky and plain before them, there was truly ' no other girl,'—that in some mysterious way, struggle as she might, contemptuous as she might outwardly seem, her fate was irrevocably bound up with his.

THERE are moments or periods, in the existence of some people, when life seems to stand still, nay, when it seems to go back; when the sequence of action seems broken, and the retribution which is supposed to dog the steps of the past deed, is, or seems to be, turned aside; when life's rivers, as some one quoted to me once, out of a Greek dramatist or poet, run backward on their courses. Such a moment occurred in the life of Blanche Boteraux. She became more and more desperate in the lovely spring weather at Clyston St. Fay. She had serious thoughts of running away. She longed to plunge herself into the stream of modern life, to enter a hospital, to join the Salvation Army, to become a Sister devoted to work in the most terrible of the London slums, to bathe her hands, as it were, in human misery, and taste the reek of its smoke that cries to Heaven. Of

all the hateful things that surrounded her in
this paradise of orchard and field and moorland
and wood, poor George Falaise was the most
hateful—his perfect politeness, his imperturba-
ble repose, the absolute indifference to everything that seemed to her worth a thought,—
she felt that if she stayed longer in this atmosphere she should go mad. Suddenly all this
was changed. Life suddenly became, in the
cant of the day, worth living, the future brilliant with a startled hope.

The way it came about was simplicity itself.
Dr. Boteraux at certain intervals attended a
Ruri-diaconal meeting. He went to these gath-
erings as he would have attended a meeting of
his college, but he did not seem to derive much
benefit from them. I fear he was not altogether
in harmony with the more active and missionary
zeal of some of his younger brethren. 'Much
irresponsible talk, my dear.' he has been known
to reply to Blanche's inquiry as to what had
occurred. I suppose it must be admitted that
the Rector of Clyston St. Fay was not a perfect
character. On his return from one of these
meetings, however, he appeared unusually interested.

'I met a gentleman who is staying with Mr.

Archdeacon — a great preacher from London, a Mr. Paul Damerle. He is in Devonshire for his health; and I have asked him to preach here on Sunday week, and to stay with us for a few days afterwards. He is said to be a very rising man, a great "missioner," as it is called, among the poor in London, and, for that matter, among the rich also.'

Blanche Boteraux's eyes glistened as she looked at her father for once with unmitigated approval.

'Did you say that he was going to preach at Clyston St Fay, sir?' said George Falaise.

'Yes. Why?'

'He won't suit your people, sir.'

'Ah, rouse them up a little, you think! God knows I should not object to that,' said the Rector mildly; 'they want something better than I can give them.'

Blanche looked up at them both with a sudden interest — at her father with an unusual sympathy, at the unfortunate boy with unutterable meaning. But, with the dogged persistence of his caste, he stuck to his text.

'I don't think so,' he said, looking down upon his plate. 'Since I came here I have heard better sermons than I have heard anywhere else; and if I only acted up to what I have heard——'

'Ah! my dear boy,' the Rector said, 'if *we* only acted up to what we *preached!*'

During the next few days more people than usual seemed to call at the Rectory, and they all spoke of the Rev. Paul Damerle. One had heard him at this place and one at another. Every one spoke of him with enthusiasm. One old lady of high rank drove twelve miles over a hill country, simply because she had been told that he was to preach at Clyston St. Fay, and to tell Blanche Boteraux that he was 'an apostolic young man.' Several clergymen who called were enthusiastic upon his work in the back slums of London. The excitement in a place where excitements were so rare became almost intense.

On the Saturday afternoon a carriage was sent to the nearest station, six miles from Clyston St. Fay, and the Rev. Paul Damerle arrived in due course, and was received by Dr. Boteraux and his daughter. George had absented himself during the whole day, and was supposed to be shooting something indefinite. They all met in the drawing-room before dinner.

The Rev. Paul Damerle was a tall and striking-looking man of twenty-seven or thirty years of age. He did not wear evening dress, but retained his ordinary attire, which was distinctly clerical, but not of an extreme type. It is difficult to say whether he could be called handsome, but he had a finely-formed, square-cut face, and strong irregular features, indicative, his admirers said, of strength, moral purpose, and intellect. The lower part of his face, which was closely shaven, was dark and massive. He looked with, apparently, some surprise at George Falaise, who was last in the room.

'Let me introduce to you Lord Falaise,' said Dr. Boteraux, 'who is reading with me before going to Oxford; the son of a very dear college friend.'

The two men bowed, but neither of them said anything.

Dr. Boteraux looked at them both with a sudden interest, as though dimly recognising that a new light had flashed upon his life.

'Mr. Damerle is enthusiastic upon the Devon air, Falaise,' he said; he generally called his pupil George. 'It will please you, as a Devon man, to hear him. He has been ill.'

'No, not ill,' said the other,—'not ill; but I felt that I was getting overwrought. The difficulties and disappointments of my work—for

there are difficulties and disappointments in such
work as mine — worried me more than they ought
to have done.'

He spoke in a full rich voice, and with a
deliberate emphasis, which gave an air of finish
and importance to what he said.

'And there were other symptoms. I have
seen so much, and heard more, of men breaking
down altogether for want of a little change. I
don't call it rest; I have no rest but in my
work.'

'You are much interested in the condition of
the working population of our large cities, I
believe,' said Dr. Boteraux politely, but with a
certain vagueness of manner, as though he were
attributing to his guest an interest in some
obscure species of carnivora with which he himself was unfamiliar.

'I am indeed deeply interested in the working
classes, and not, I hope, in them only, but in my
fellow-beings everywhere, and in all that may
promote their wellbeing.'

There was perhaps the faintest appearance of
rhetoric in Damerle's tone as he said this, but
there was also an unmistakable sincerity in it.
It is a necessity of the case that the devoted
preacher, or teacher of religion, must drop some-

thing of the reserve on such matters which distinguishes the ordinary layman.

Blanche listened, though it would have been difficult for her to have told why, with an excitement which she had not felt for many months, perhaps never before. She sat looking from one to another of her companions with an interest not less intense. It was a curious fact that the arrival of this new acquaintance stirred and enhanced her relationship to the old. They each acted as foil and contrast to the other, and by their conduct and by the apparent effect of the new arrival upon the others, she seemed better able to appreciate his personality herself.

She sat looking from Damerle to George Falaise, as they stood side by side upon the hearth. I doubt whether she had ever looked at George so much, or been so interested in him before. She found indeed, with a startled feeling of inward annoyance, that instead of suffering by the comparison with this brilliant and devoted stranger, the boy perceptibly grew in appearance, and even, stranger than all, in her estimation.

He was elaborately dressed. It may seem to some that there is not much scope for difference in an Englishman's evening dress, but it is not so.   There are niceties and curiosities which, though she knew nothing about them, her female instinct taught her to perceive and to appreciate. As he stood upon the white hearth-skin, his steadfast eyes fixed searchingly upon Damerle — the quiet perfection of his dress combining with the exquisite setting of that quaint room around him — it was impossible to be unconscious of his attraction, or of the natural distinction of his mien and pose.   He was not quite so tall as the other, and he was some ten years younger, but the gifts of heredity and rank more than compensated for these disadvantages, if such they might be called.   But the striking if, as some might think, subtle contrast between the two men lay in the expression of the face.   In the set curves of George Falaise's small delicately-cut mouth, and in the look of his singularly beautiful eyes, there was a certain steadfastness which was wanting in the other.   It is true that the lower part of Paul Damerle's face conveyed the impression of great strength, but it was the strength of obstinacy more than of steadfastness; while his eyes, which were dark and very fine, had a far-off look of intensity which made them almost expressionless.   In a word, it might be said of the two men, that while Damerle gave

the impression of vast and unknown possibilities
in the moral universe, with an equally undefin-
able future, you felt of George Falaise that, with
fewer or perhaps no possibilities, you could safely
divine what, within the limits of his moral vision,
he would most certainly do. About the determined lines of Damerle's face there was a lurking tendency to exasperation, to combativeness,
which was perfectly absent from the assured
serenity of George Falaise's look and manner.

Blanche felt a curious irritation rising within
her against the boy, excited by this undeniable
advance which he had made in her perception of
him. If he would only have made a fool of
himself in some way, or otherwise manifested
his inferiority, she would have felt much more
kindly towards him. But George Falaise had
evidently no intention of doing anything of the
kind; in fact he did nothing, and, with the exception of a short answer to a question of the
Rector's as to his shooting, he said nothing.
The composed observant silence with which he
stood fascinated Blanche, and became intolerable
to her. She felt something of that sense of an
impending fate that linked her to him, which
she had felt in descending from the moor. The
feeling terrified and exasperated her, and, with

the power of a determined nature, she set herself resolutely to defy and to combat it.

In the excitement of this feeling she had for a moment forgotten Mr. Damerle, but now she was roused to attention by his voice, speaking with its deep rich tone —

'As Dr. Liddon says, they strangle us in luxurious drawing-rooms with a silken thread. We are welcome so long as we prophesy smooth things, but the moment we speak the truth — the moment we speak to them as

'"Sinners in a world of care" —

the moment we tell them of the world of misery and of sin, seething and smouldering at their very doors, — then they give us the cold shoulder, then they call us Enthusiasts, Socialists, Romanists, Ultramontanes. Therefore we turn to the poor. The Lord was poor.'

Blanche Boteraux's face flushed with excitement and delight at these words, accordant as they were to the suppressed and buried life within her. Dr. Boteraux looked slightly puzzled, like a massive ironclad attacked by a torpedo boat from an unexpected quarter. Irritated, apparently, by something that seemed implied in Damerle's words or tone, George

Falaise put his foot in it in a quite unlooked-for way.

'I know nothing of the working classes,' he said; 'but I know something of the upper—my godfather is a duke—and I think their view is that no permanent good would arise by their giving up their present style of living and slumming it.'

Blanche regarded him almost with affection. The spell was broken. He had displayed his inferiority now without any doubt.

Mr. Damerle looked at him with an indulgent smile, as though he would have said, 'That is exactly the sentiment I should have expected from a young man brought up as you have been. Let us hope that you will learn better.'

Fortunately, perhaps, at this moment dinner was announced.

The conversation at dinner was sustained almost entirely by Damerle. Blanche asked a few questions and listened with her whole soul. The Rector was unusually silent. The anecdotes and epigrams were not forthcoming. There was no one present to whom they were new except the guest, and probably the Rector thought that they would not be appreciated by him. George, having fired off his little artillery in defence of his order, appeared to consider that he had satisfied the exigencies of the occasion, and confined his attention to the dinner and to the Rector's excellent La Rose.

It must be admitted that Damerle talked exceedingly well. He was evidently a man of wide culture and reading, who had trained himself to utilise everything that he had read and heard. History, literature, description of scenery, humorous anecdotes even, had all been stored for use both in sermons and conversation. When the Rector, emboldened by some of his guest's anecdotes, ventured upon one or two of the best of his own, Damerle evidently transferred them to his mental tablet. All his conversation, however, centred itself ultimately in his work and his mission, — 'his Master's service,' as he boldly said. The sense of this was never lost. If a cynic had been asked, he might possibly have said that 'the Master's service' centred itself somewhat in the Rev. Paul Damerle, but a cynic will say anything. I suppose that the Apostle Paul was ambitious of promoting his Master's service, and in this sense Paul Damerle was undoubtedly ambitious. A laudable aspiration you will say, no doubt, but it would seem that it has the germ of some insidious mischief in it which may be the initial if not the immediate cause of a terrible fall. When a man once suffers himself to imagine that he is necessary to God, the power to resist temptations is manifestly much lessened and their force proportionally increased.

Towards the middle of dinner George committed himself again, and this time got a decided fall.

Some remark brought up the Salvation Army. Damerle spoke warmly in its praise — speaking of the improvement its efforts had produced in low districts, and quoting the testimony of the police.

'But the Salvation bonnet?' George broke in.

'The title sounds strange to us, doubtless,' said Damerle quietly; 'but I confess that I see little difference in phrase between "Salvation bonnet" and "Collar of the Sancto Spirito" — one of the greatest orders in Europe, I believe; you know better than I.' And he looked full into George's face as if for confirmation. The boy looked very blank.

'Awfully clever remark that of his,' he said innocently to Blanche the next day. — 'that about the Salvation bonnet and the Collar of S.S. It floored me.'

After dinner Blanche played some sacred airs. When she had finished, and they were saying good-night, Mr. Damerle said —

· You were speaking at dinner, Miss Boteraux, of Frédéric Amiel. He says somewhere, I remember, that music carries us to heaven, because music is harmony, harmony is perfection, perfection is our dream, and our dream is Heaven. I rather think it is because music is a voice. Men, even the worst of us, seek direction; they seek a Divine Voice.'

'The Romans,' said the Rector, ' erected an altar to Aius Locutius, a warning voice.'

'A voice crying in the wilderness,' said Damerle, ' "Prepare ye the way of the Lord." '

Outside the drawing-room, as Blanche left it, there was a sudden hush and chill.

She passed a wide hall dimly lighted, from which a long rambling wooden staircase, with many turnings, led to the upper rooms.

As Blanche went up the staircase alone, those last words of her father rang in her ears with a strange attraction, with a freshness and intensity which pagan thought sometimes brings: ' An altar to Aius Locutius, a warning voice.' Her father could have told her that Cicero complains that the voice spoke but once.

'We seek direction; we seek a Divine Voice,' Damerle had said; and as she thought of it, at the same moment, her recollection went back, in spite of herself as it were, in the still gloomy shadow of the wide staircase, to George Falaise, standing upon the white hearth-skin, the honest steady look in the beautiful eyes, the perfect pose, the faultless dress. She thrust the vision from her with a ruthless determination. Was it possible that she refused to listen to a warning voice?

V

The entire population of Clyston St. Fay attended church on Sunday mornings. What became of the village on a Sunday morning, or what happened to the Sunday dinners, I do not know, I never could find out; but the above may be taken as the statement of a literal fact. On the Sunday morning, therefore, on which Mr. Damerle preached, there was no very perceptible difference in the appearance of the congregation. There were a few stragglers from neighbouring villages present, but that was all.

The Rector read the prayers and the second lesson. The Rector was an excellent reader. George Falaise said that he was the best in England, but perhaps poor George's dictum will not be taken as conclusive. At any rate Dr. Boteraux's reading was that of a scholar and a gentleman trained in long practice of elocution. Then Damerle preached.

I do not suppose that such a sermon had ever been heard at Clyston St. Fay since the Normans built a church there. He took for his text the mystic words of the Apocalypse: 'And the Spirit and the bride say, Come, and let him that heareth say, Come.'

'From the primeval chaos, when the Eternal Word swept across the tremulous ether and the wastes of uncreated yet instinctive life, through successive generations, as the Divine prompting strove with men with alluring yet insistent voice, to the time when, in mystery which was from the beginning, "proceeding forth, yet leaving not the Father's side," the Word was made flesh, and dwelt among us,—through all this wonderful story, pleading and striving with all men, with peasants and with kings, with pagans and with Christians, with freemen and with slaves, with those who clothe in fine linen, and pride themselves as the cultured and refined of earth, and with those who have not where to lay their head, permeating through all ranks, effluent through all culture, as Scevola the Pontifex is said by St. Augustine to have disputed of a theology which was at once that of poets, and philosophers, and princes of cities; through evil report and good report, as deceivers and yet true, we beseech you to think of these things.

'To this pleading voice, following us into every trivial incident, as we speak of triviality, of our daily life, let us give heed; and having given heed, what remains for us to do?

'"Let him that heareth say, Come."

'This is the return demanded from every one who has tasted of the heavenly gift. "Lord, send me!" Was this our longing, and was this our cry, to surrender ourselves to His service, to follow Him whithersoever He may lead?'

Something like this was the idea of the sermon that remained in Blanche's mind as she came out of church.

She had sat with George Falaise alone in the old rectory pew — Blanche in the corner next the door, from whence she could best see the preacher, George in the opposite angle of the long pew, exactly under the pulpit. His attitude was one of studied and profound indifference, but he heard every word. Blanche, on the contrary, had kept her eyes fixed upon the preacher with an appearance of rapt attention.

They came out together, Blanche a little in advance. They did not say anything for some time, walking up the village street, boy and girl like, in the sulks.   Then Blanche, feeling certain that her companion, with reprobate perversity, would disapprove, but probably thinking that her conduct was not consistent with the preacher's advice, turned round towards George and said—

'What did you think of the sermon?   Was it not wonderful?'

His face flushed all over with a boyish determination to speak the truth at all hazard.

'I thought it awfully bad form, in your father's presence too.'

It would take a three-volume novel of the modern realistic school of character-analysis to explain what he meant, but it seems hardly worth the while; Blanche certainly did not trouble herself to that extent.

There was no more said between the two until they reached the rectory.

The Rector came up with Damerle, but entered the drawing-room alone.

'Great sermon!' he said.   'Wealth of illustration surprising in so short a time! Widely-read man, and knows how to use his reading! Very much pleased.   Don't wonder the people run after him!'

Upon the congregation the sermon practically produced no effect—no effect at all.

' Suthin' like t' Methodist rant, weren't it ? ' one or two of the elder farmers said to Mr. Churchwarden Wike in their soft, flowing Devon tongue. Mr. Wike shook his head seriously but said nothing. Mrs. Churchwarden was more outspoken.

' Nuthin' good enough for him, I should say,' she said ; 'and that stuck-up Miss Boteraux thinks so too, for I watched her. They had better marry and go away together, and a good riddance, I should say. We did very well with t' old Rector before either of them came.'

I have looked through Blanche Boteraux's diary carefully to find any mention of this sermon or of Mr. Damerle, but without success. The only mention of Damerle occurs once.

' Mr. Damerle ' (without any introduction, for he has never been mentioned before) ' was speaking at dinner about Wesley. He said that at the beginning of his journals he enters into a long argument in favour of instantaneous conversion and assurance — a doctrine which, Mr. Damerle says, he got from the Moravians, but which he thought that Wesley never altogether appropriated. After a warm and enthusiastic argument Wesley concludes with what Mr.

Damerle thinks the most beautiful sentence ever written. Instead of hurling anathemas on the presumptuous person who would differ from the great teacher, he says —

' " If any man cannot receive this, let him pray for more light, both for him and for me." '

A little further down the page she says: 'I did not quite know why Mr. Damerle spoke of the Moravians as though he did not like them, and I asked him if he had seen the *Life of Nicholas Lewis, Count Zinzendorf*, which had been given to me as a prize at Neufchâtel, and which I always thought was a most beautiful book, and read more than almost any other. He did not seem to know much about it. I showed him one of my favourite passages, which sounds so beautiful in the German —

' " His intentions were briefly these : Faithfully to take charge of poor souls, for whom Christ had shed His blood, and especially to collect together and to protect those that were oppressed and persecuted. He had also in view the fellowship of the children of God; and he endeavoured by all means to promote love and unanimity amongst those who were awakened and called to the kingdom of God." '

' Mr. Damerle seemed pleased with this. He smiled and said, " Yes ; *briefly* these ! " '

A little further on I find the following, from Walker of Truro, which I think that Mr. Damerle must have suggested to her, and which I quote, because it seems to me to be in accord with the peculiarly optimistic view which he took of his mission and of himself. But in any case the passage is a fine one, as expressing a kind of abstract gratitude which any man may feel for what he conceives to have been peculiar blessings in his lot.

'"He" (the writer is speaking of the Christian) "owns His hand both in the visitations of Chastisement and Prosperity, seeing Love in them both. Confirmed he is that his soul is God's special care, while with grateful wonder he reflects upon God's forbearance and gentleness towards him. The wise and strange means and contrivances God hath used with him; the kind disappointments, and most inviting encouragements he hath met with from Him; in a word, the long and watchful discipline which an affectionate Providence hath exercised upon him." '

Mr. Damerle remained four or five days at Clyston St. Fay. I am inclined to think that they were days too bright almost for remembrance, not to say for writing down; at any rate we find no trace of them in the diary. When he left, the weeks and months at the rectory seem to have been very dull and flat. There are no quotations, and no record of any events.

There are lapses in life, times of deferred hope that seems disappointment, of depression that borders on the scepticism of despair; they follow mostly on periods of excitement and of special insight and illumination. On such occasions what can the historian do? If all is dead and chill in the time and in the life recorded, what can be said of such a time or such a life? It was under the shadow of such a cloud — I imagine to myself — that Blanche Boteraux entered when Mr. Damerle had left the rectory. In love with Paul Damerle, in the vulgar sense of the phrase, it scarcely needs to say she was not. Indeed, it is more than doubtful whether she ever saw the real Paul Damerle at all. What she saw was a creature of her own fancy, of her own spiritual need, of the guiding instinct of her life. Yet, though to speak of her as in any vulgar sense in love with Damerle were ridiculous and even libellous, the absorption of her nature into his, the attraction of her spirit towards the ideal which she associated with his presence and action, was more imperative and complete than any ordinary attraction could possibly be.

It seemed to her young consciousness that she had found the complement and answer to all incompleteness and want, to all the questionings, to all the inadequateness of life; and when nothing happened, nothing followed upon this glorious dawn and promise of a pledged future, rich in blessings more to others than to herself, there settled down upon Blanche's life, at the rectory, a dulness, if not a darkness, that might be felt. Yet, true to the guiding instinct even under the shadow of death, she evidently set her face towards that goal which had been revealed to her as the end of life — the goal of self-denial and of sacrifice. When Heaven's light has been revealed for a moment, it is not easy to sink back into the paltry half-tints of commonplace existence.

Dr. Boteraux took them up to Oxford at the beginning of the Easter term; I suppose he thought that it was time that George went there. Blanche does not appear to have thought much of Oxford. She makes some remarks in her diary which, for her sake, I think it best to suppress. To a restless disturbed spirit, young and untrained in life's story, it is of little avail to talk of shady walks, of smooth grassy courts, of mellow, ivy-covered walls and oriels, instinct with the life of past days. These things are nothing in regard to it. Blanche mentions very briefly in her diary some little excitements — afternoon teas and the Doctor's dining in Hall in more than one college — but, on the whole, Oxford did not seem to have interested her.

She relates, however, at considerable length an incident which may not seem important, but which had evidently taken her fancy.

A gentleman said to her at afternoon tea: 'Will you introduce me to your brother, Miss Boteraux?'

'My brother?'

'Yes; the young man who is standing by your father, whom you called George.'

'Oh, Lord Falaise! he is not my brother; but it is an excellent idea. I will tell him.'

Accordingly, on the first opportunity, she said: 'George, a gentleman asked me just now if you were my brother. That is just what we ought to be. I will be your sister always.'

I can see it all, — her look as she said those words, the bewitching fascination of her brown eyes and of her smile — she had not lost her smile then — the bewilderingly exasperating effect upon George Falaise, her utter unconsciousness of the effect she wrought.

For once he forgot himself.

'No, you won't,' he said.

She tells no more; but I have sometimes thought that, as she turned away, thus repulsed, there came into her eyes, for the first time, something of a look that, in the years that were to come, I was to know so well.

VI

Clyston St. Fay was at its stillest in the
early summer days. The visit to Oxford had
not been without its results. George Falaise
commenced his residence at St. Nod's very soon
after. It might seem that the recollection even
of past excitement had faded away. That sis-
terly love — surely a precious thing, and not to
be despised, which she had freely offered, and
which had been rudely refused — is it possible
that it might have grown, in this soft, flower-
scented hush and sweetness, into something
more? 'Les absens ont toujours tort?' Ah no!
It is the present, with its vulgar insistence,
its blunders. its stupid compliments, its mistaken
bonhomie, that is in the wrong. The absent, who,
silent themselves, let those others speak for them
— the remorse, the pathos of the past — the
terribly regretted past — the mistaken word, the
misjudged action, the hasty quarrel irrevocable
now — the absent in the wrong! Ah no!

98

However this may be, in this case the lethargy, the hush and pause which gave the soul time to think, and which might, had fate willed, have been the prelude and tilth of a happy spring and healthy fruitage, was suddenly broken in upon. Mr. Damerle appeared again. He came quite unexpectedly one afternoon when the Rector was out visiting a sick parishioner.

The Rector was very great in visiting the sick. His method was very simple, and whatever might have been thought of it elsewhere, was exceedingly admired at Clyston St. Fay. He would enter the sickroom with a very kindly and cheery manner; then he would begin to talk of the weather or of the crops, of any cheerful event in the village, such as a marriage, or a birth in the family; then he would draw the patient out to talk a little about himself or herself, — a great secret of success; then he would say —

'Would you like me to read to you two or three good prayers?'

These he would read from a selection which he had made himself, interspersed with some passages of Scripture, and pasted into a book, bound in morocco, with the sacred monogram in silver on the outside. Most of his sick parishioners would say that he was better than the village doctor. One old lady who was on the point of death, given over by the doctor, went so far as to recover, and was at work again in forty-eight hours. This event perfectly established the Rector's reputation. The mothers would say —

'My lad's very sick, your honour; would you come and read a prayer over him?' And it is possible that He who raised the widow of Nain's son was not deaf to the Rector's prayers, though they were read out of a morocco-bound book, with a silver monogram.

On this particular afternoon the sick parishioner lay in a remote outskirt of the parish, and the Rector was away for a long time.

Blanche was walking in the old-fashioned garden under the terraced hedges, beneath the stately Queen Anne front. There was a dulcet blue in the Devon sky, an enervating softness in the Devon air, that soothed the restlessness of her heart, and accorded more with the idea of George Falaise than with that of Paul Damerle. But in that moment, in the rest and stillness of the golden afternoon, it was Paul Damerle and not George Falaise who came down the mossy stone steps suddenly upon her.

Damerle, with his apostolic fervour, and his

quite sincere devotion. was after all only a man;
he had come back with some vague desire, some
unformed wish. He wanted to see again that
young stately mien, to look again into those
earnest-speaking eyes, to hear again that serious
speech that seemed neither to brook nor to
understand anything but what was noble and
unselfish and high. When he came into the
garden he had no other thought than this, but
the glamour of the hour, and his surprised
delight at her young beauty. hurried him on.
She looked astonishingly beautiful in the flush
of embarrassment and surprise. It seemed to
Damerle that a new light had suddenly burst
upon his path — that path which he had hitherto
looked upon — nay, gloried in looking upon —
as the path of self-denial and renunciation.
The path was still there; it led to the same
results. He felt the same impulses, the same
ideal stirred him. but an altogether strange and
delightful personality seemed added to his life
and to the future of his work. By one of those
coincidences so frequent in life, the lines from
The Princess, which Blanche had copied, came
into his mind —

> 'Woman is not undeveloped man,
>   But diverse.'

The sudden rush of feeling and of impulse was so overpowering that he forgot the ordinary greetings of social life, and stood on the grassy verge below the terrace, face to face with Blanche Boteraux, looking at her without a word.

It was she who recovered self-possession first.

'I did not know that you were come back, Mr. Damerle,' she said.

A certain change took place in Damerle's sensation as she spoke, for her words threw him back at once upon the exigencies of ordinary life. He saw that he had placed himself on the horns of a dilemma from which it seemed to him he had but one exit. He had no possible excuse but one for coming back. His nature was intensely dramatic, and this tendency had been still further exaggerated by culture in Greek classics and by the necessities of the pulpit. It was his temptation to feel that the right thing to do at the moment was the dramatically correct thing. He would not himself have phrased it in these words. He would have spoken of it as 'a higher leading,' as 'an instinctive call,' 'a flash of illumination from above'; but whether he knew it or not, the dramatic instinct was the spring of his action always.

Still he did not speak. He stood looking at
Blanche Boteraux with those great expressionless eyes that had almost a magnetic power.
It would have been impossible for any conduct
to have been contrived which would have greater
effect. She felt dazed and bewildered, as with
the expectation of some coming shock. In the
weary years afterwards she remembered that
time, that summer afternoon, those fleeting
moments that, with no seeking of her own, and
apparently with no foreseen intention of another,
decided the issues of her life, the fine shingle
path on which she stood, the grassy terrace, the
fuchsia hedges that clothed the terrace walls,
the fir branches that skirted the garden down
the village road, the misty sunlight, the soft
afternoon air, an overruling stillness and calm,
and expectant hush of sense, — long afterwards
she remembered them all.

At last he spoke.

'I have come back, Miss Boteraux,' he said, in a
measured, perfectly self-possessed, and melodious
tone, 'because I could not keep away. It has been
shown me very clearly, since I was here, what
has been wanting to me, — the want and the craving I have been vaguely conscious of — the want
which has rendered my work both less successful

and infinitely more trying and wearing to myself.
At the very birth of the race it was perceived by
the Divine Wisdom that it was not well for man
to be alone.   A helpmeet was provided for him,
who

> '" is not undeveloped man,
> But diverse.
> Till at the last she set herself to man,
> As perfect music unto noble words,
> Yoked in all exercise of noble end."

'Blanche! will you be this perfect music to
me?'

It would have been difficult to have chosen
words, forced and unnatural as they may seem to
some people, or a manner and tone, cold and collected as the pleading might seem, which would
have impressed Blanche Boteraux so much as
Damerle's words and manner did.   The tone of
voice, it is true, was unbroken and calm, but it
was solemn, and even intensely earnest.

It was a manner and a pleading very different
doubtless from that of George Falaise, and for
this reason perhaps it impressed Blanche all the
more.   She was as yet only a girl, and her experience of the world, which seemed so convincing
and so satisfying to her, was scarcely adequate,
perhaps, to guide her in the most fatal moments
of her life.   The recurrence of her favourite pas-

sage from *The Princess* struck her as with a solemn surprise. The whole address seemed to come to her with a well-recognised tone, as from a world with which she was familiar. The proposal came to her as one which fulfilled all the aspirations of her young life — the conception of the most desirable the most perfect future that she had ever formed. A thrill of feeling, which amounted almost to ecstasy at this realised hope, at this fulfilled desire, passed through her frame, and her face flushed and her eyes brightened with a strange light; nevertheless, she did not for a second lose the reserved air, the girlish stateliness, which was hers by natural gift.

She looked at him steadily with the serious, far-reaching gaze of her hazel eyes, to which the sudden flash of light only gave a deeper intenseness and a more searching power.

Damerle felt a sudden chill beneath those searching eyes that seemed to penetrate to the depths of his existence. What they might find there, he could not answer for. He knew not what was there himself.

'It is very sudden, Mr. Damerle,' she said, 'and I am quite alone. Let us go down the village. We shall meet my father as we go.'

It was not what he had expected, though

what he had expected he hardly knew. He had no alternative but to accede to her proposal, but he followed her with a sense of unexpected repulse, which only added zest to his desire.

They went down the deeply sunken village road, between the sharp-cut walls of natural rock, supporting the small terraces and garden plots upon which the cottages were built, in every variety of picturesque outline and form. The whitewashed walls of the cottages, covered with creeping roses, and honeysuckle, and clematis, and passion-flower, and the rock, partly whitewashed with the cottages, and partly covered with lichen and hart's-tongue and oak-fern, contrasted with the hedges of fuchsias, and myrtle, and veronica, and valerian, shining in the moisture of the recent shower and in the brightness of the afternoon sun.

They said very little, even nothing, as they went down the village road. Damerle could not help wondering how silenced he was in the presence of this girl — he who had generally so much to say for himself. He found himself, strangely enough, at such a time thrown back upon himself. He felt a strange necessity laid upon him to look well into his secret heart, and to make quite sure what his motives and inten-

tions were. It was somewhat of a new experience. He had been so accustomed to take the
Rev. Paul Damerle for granted. In the searching light of those hazel eyes everything was
changed, the platitudes of existence had no
dwelling there.

Near the bottom of the village, by the church,
they met the Rector walking slowly up the road.

Blanche went up to her father with a most
unwonted look and gesture, and hung upon his
arm. The Rector was a man of the world. He
was very tired after his long walk in the afternoon sun, but he knew exactly what had occurred
as minutely as if he had been present and had
heard every word that had been spoken.

'Ah! Mr. Damerle,' he said, 'you have come
back. Very glad to see you. You will stay the
night of course.'

Now the pleasantest thing in life that could
have occurred to Dr. Boteraux would have been
that his daughter should have married George
Falaise. Apart from the brilliancy of the match,
from a worldly point of view, he had become
very fond of this fascinating boy, who had
attached himself, with something of a canine
fidelity, to his tutor and his host. But very
serious considerations were involved in the idea

of such an alliance. Dr. Boteraux had not had the slightest scruple in asking three hundred pounds, or in accepting five hundred when it was sent him, as an equivalent for George's visit and tuition; but he would have had the very greatest hesitation in promoting, or even consenting to, the marriage of his daughter to Lord Falaise, unless he was perfectly certain that his guardian, the Duke, cordially approved of it. He could hardly suppose that this would be the case. His mind was, therefore, reduced to a position of absolute suspense. He felt himself growing old. and life and the future were uncertain. His pecuniary troubles had told upon him. Damerle might not prove a bad match. He had fancied that his daughter was attracted towards him; her manner even now was strange to him, and there was a light in her eyes which he never remembered to have seen before. He would do nothing hastily; he would wait and see.

They walked up the village street side by side. Damerle was strangely silent, but that rather impressed the Rector favourably in regard to him. He spoke first.

'Have you seen the Archdeacon since you left us, Mr. Damerle?' he said.

'No, I have been at Plymouth preaching — a

sort of mission. There is a great work doing in the " Three Towns," and not, I suppose, before it was needed.'

They walked on in silence. The sense that something was occurring of mysterious importance which kept them silent was not felt by themselves alone. The whole village shared it. There were, at that hour of the afternoon, only women and children and one or two old men at home, but the whole village life, such as it was, was stirred. The little children, even, gazed at the group with more than usual awe, and 'ole grandfer Elsworthy,' who rarely stirred from the seat by his cottage door, grasped his stick with a set purpose, and tottering to the edge of his little domain, stood trembling on the verge of the garden precipice, gazing eagerly after the trio, when they had passed up the road.

When they had reached the house, and he had shown Damerle to his room, the Rector went into the drawing-room to his daughter.

She was standing in front of the bay window, looking out at the deer and the grassy park; she turned as he came in and looked him full in the face. As he looked into her eyes he knew something which he had only guessed at before. His mind was quite made up.

'So Mr. Damerle has proposed to you, my dear,' he said.

She had, in truth, never seen his face before. There had been moments when the kindly, fatherly look had won her child's heart, and had assured her of a home, and of help upon earth, but never before had she known her father as he was.

In the worn, clever face, in the deeply-cut features, and the delicately-drawn lines which seemed to have retained the trace of insight and knowledge and culture — the culture of past worlds — she read now something more. She saw through the mask, as it were, of this face, strange to her in one sense, though in another so familiar, — strange in its associations with a life and a scholarship alien to her nature and to her training — a yearning, a fatherly, natural, and, were it possible, a protecting love.

'So Mr. Damerle has proposed to you, my dear,' he said.

'Yes, how did you know? Has he told you?'

'No; he has not said a word. I knew it the moment I met you in the village. What did you say to him?'

'I told him that it was very sudden — that I

was alone, and that we had better go to meet you.'

'And what shall you tell him?'

She paused for a moment, then passed the question by.

'It has made me very happy,' she said.

'You love him, then?'

Again she did not answer his question.

'He is so noble and good,' she said, 'so devoted to his work, and such work! It is what I have longed for, but scarcely dared to hope. To be taken by such a man, trained to such a work, aided, supported, made necessary even to him. Can there be a prouder lot, a more glorious fate?'

He looked at her for a moment fondly, and with a sort of admiration, which, in truth, was not surprising, as she stood in the flush of her enthusiasm, the light in her face ennobling what was, even without it, a face and girlish form such as some men would have gone far to have seen but once.

He looked at her for a moment, then he said —

'Blanche, did George Falaise ever speak to you?'

'Yes, father, but only as a boy. I told him it

could never be. It was only a few words, or I
would have told you.'

He looked at her a little sadly for a moment,
as though dismissing a hope, then he said, very
kindly —

'Well, if you have quite decided, I con-
gratulate you, my dear. I shall speak to Mr.
Damerle, and then send him to you; there is
something that I must say to him first.'

The Rector sent Binns up to Mr. Damerle's
room to ask him, when he came downstairs,
to go to Dr. Boteraux's study, and in a few
moments he was shown in. The Rector had
evidently arranged for the interview. He was
seated in an armchair, with its back to the
window, reading; but he had placed another
armchair opposite to him in a position in which
he could see the occupant's face distinctly. He
rose as Damerle came in and motioned him into
this seat. Damerle sat down.

'My daughter tells me, Mr. Damerle,' said
the Rector, 'that you have made her a proposal
of marriage. I shall wish her to give you an
answer herself; but, before she does so, there are
some things which I must speak to you about.
I should have much preferred,' he went on, 'if
you had given me an opportunity of saying

these things before you had spoken to my daughter. I have had no such opportunity given me, and therefore the blame can in no case be laid upon me. You may not suppose it, Mr. Damerle, but I am a poor man; were I to die to-morrow, my daughter in all probability would have absolutely nothing.'

He paused for a moment, but probably thinking that he should take an unfair advantage of his companion were he to stop suddenly after so startling an announcement, he went on again.

' Circumstances, which I need not more particularly explain, have prevented my coming into possession of a large property, which at one time I had every reason to suppose would be mine, and my right to it has been disputed ever since. Judgment has been given against me. It has been appealed against, and the final decision will not long be delayed. The probability is that the judgment of the inferior court will be confirmed. If that be the case, the position of my daughter will be as I have stated.'

He looked steadily into Damerle's face, upon which the evening light was shining strongly, but he learned very little there. The expressionless eyes were as striking and as reticent as ever,

and if the corners of the set mouth were drawn
a little lower down than usual, this only gave an
expression of increased earnestness to the face,
which the occasion would amply justify. But in
fact no very great struggle was going on in
Damerle's mind. He may have felt some timid
shrinking, as of a man who had made a mistake,
or had been, at the least, somewhat precipitate,
for after a great and decisive action it is not
uncommon, in the reaction that follows upon
excitement, for the mind and will to shrink a
little from the possible consequences of their
deed. He had not proposed to Blanche Boteraux
with any mercenary thought or motive, but
simply as carried onward by, in some degree,
a sudden impulse and attraction. Even the
hardest and most cynical man would have found
it difficult to make such a proposal as he had
made and retract it in a single day, and Damerle
was far from being such a man. He was neither
hard nor cynical. He was a man of lofty and
even strained ideals ; and if there was weakness
and failure in his nature, which led to these
ideals not being always adequately achieved, it
will probably occur to most of us that in this he
did not stand alone.

He was an intensely receptive man. There

was something in the evident chivalric determination of Dr. Boteraux not to lose a moment in
explaining his circumstances to the man who
was seeking his daughter's hand which appealed
to his imagination, and for the moment dominated all other impression, seeming to demand a
corresponding action on his part. He rose from
his seat and spoke at once, with scarcely a
moment's pause.

'I may regret what you have told me, Dr.
Boteraux. for your daughter's sake, for my own
means are very limited indeed; otherwise, what
you have told me can make no difference in my
intentions. I am far too strongly attracted to
your daughter by feelings of the warmest admiration and respect for such considerations to
have any influence. At the same time, I am
bound to add that if, after what you have told
me, and after what I am forced to confess
myself, that I have practically no income but
that which I may receive for clerical work,
you should consider, as you very naturally may,
that I am not justified in pursuing my suit to
your daughter, I am willing to leave this house
at once, and never mention the subject to her
again.'

The Rector sat still for a moment looking

into the fire. Damerle sat down again. It was a curious pause. What answer Damerle wished for I cannot say, perhaps he himself at the moment hardly knew. Dr. Boteraux would have given all he had to have taken his visitor at his word, but he dared not do it. The light in his daughter's eyes forbade him. It was too late.

That solemn yet mostly unnoticed beat, continuous in many rooms for more than one lifetime, with a mechanism which becomes almost sympathetic with mind, had repeated some thirty warning strokes, and the moment of decision was past for ever.

'I cannot take upon myself to say that,' said the Rector. 'You had better see my daughter. She is very young, but she is older in mind than in years. She must decide for herself.'

Thus thrown upon his own resources, Damerle had no course open to him but to meet the consequences of his action as best he might. An intensely intellectual man, no single incident of the last few hours, no one characteristic of the situation, was lost upon him. It may seem strange to some people, but it is a fact that in this quiet house, with this father and daughter, he, the missioner to all classes, felt himself nerved to a higher life, to a more perfect reality of action than that which ordinarily prompted him. It is one thing to preach constantly to others, it is quite another thing, in every detail of daily life, to act as we shall one day most surely wish that we had acted. Damerle was far too clever a man not to know this.

He paused for a moment at the drawing room door, then he opened it and went in. Blanche had apparently been walking up and down the room, but she was standing in the window as he entered, and turned as he came in. The position was a fortunate one for her. The outlines of her figure, thrown up against the quaint sashes of the bay-window, stood out in strong and attractive relief. Damerle stood silent for a moment in the centre of the room before he spoke.

'Miss Boteraux,' he said, 'before I say anything else, I must say one thing. I must acknowledge that I have made a great mistake. Your own instinct told you so the moment I had spoken in the garden, and your father has clearly shown me that such is the fact. I should have spoken to your father before I ventured to address my hopes and my aspirations to you. Your father has shown me that in accepting me you probably devote yourself to a life of poverty, of deprivation, of self-denial in every form. Had I known what he has told me, I should certainly have hesitated before I had dared to ask you to link your lot with mine. But you have given no answer; more than that, my proposition evidently came upon you with a shock of surprise. I trust, therefore, that my unguarded impulse has not been productive of irrevocable mischief. With all the earnestness of which I am capable I renew my request. I feel that there is something in you in which I am most deficient — something that will brace me to higher effort, to a purer walk with God; nevertheless, I am bound to tell you that, as far as I can judge from his manner, your father, though leaving you absolutely unfettered, is not desirous that you should marry me. I have made a mistake, but I hope that, as far as in me lies, I have rectified it now.'

He had advanced into the room as he spoke and was standing where he could see her face. She had retreated to one side and was standing against the faded curtains, as if at bay; her hands clasped before her, her head thrown

back, and her eyes fixed steadfastly upon his.
' Poverty, deprivation, self-denial in every form!'
What words were these to use to her!—to her,
whose one aspiration in life included, as an absolute necessity, every one of these things.   The
unfortunate and indiscreet, though well-inten-
tioned, allusion to her father struck her at the
heart.   Was her father, then, while outwardly
kind and sympathetic, secretly leagued against
her and her highest good?   She hardened her
heart and set her face against her foes, temporal
and spiritual, visible and invisible, on every side.

She was a magnificent creature, in the splendour of pose and figure, with the strongly-cut
feminine young face, with the quivering vitality
and *verve*, before which suffering and poverty
and death were as nothing, and the paltry halt-
ings and conventionalities of life were trodden
under foot, not with any effort or consciousness,
but with a sort of involuntary action, as though
the very existence of such things was unknown
to her.   A creature to be won, if so it might be,
at all risks and all hazards; so it must seem to
any one worthy of the name of man!

' I am not afraid of poverty,' she said.

There was a sort of magnetic power about
her that attracted him with irresistible force.

It almost seemed to him, as he gazed upon her, that he saw before him the reality of all his preaching — at once the outcome and the object of his faith. Her self-abandonment and her faith seemed at the same moment both to fulfil and to shame all the words that he had ever uttered upon Faith and upon Hope.

He stood looking at her, and the expressionless eyes for once told their story only too well.

He might have seemed to other girls a cold and backward lover, but he did not seem such to this girl. She would have shrunk with repugnance, approaching to terror, from any familiarity of personal contact, from any warmth even of expression. What she sought, what she loved, was not so much the man as the man's faith, — his innermost life, his very being, his soul itself.

He held out both his hands. 'If you will take me,' he said, 'we will work together the work of God.'

She gave him both her hands.

For the next few weeks there is much to be gleaned from Blanche Boteraux's diary, not in the way of any record of occurrences, for such things she never seemed to enter, but because I find passages which, at any rate in the light of after events, seem to me at least to indicate what was passing in her life.

'It makes me tremble,' she writes, 'to think how perfectly what *I* wished and what *I* planned has been given to me. How often are we told that God sees not as we see, and that what we ignorantly wish for, He, in mercy, withholds. But everything that I wished for, everything that I felt to be the highest and the best, is mine: given me in the most surprising, the most unlooked-for way. What can I do to deserve such gracious treatment? How can I possibly live so as not to discredit it? Some plentiful harvest, some great future (it seems impossible, nay faithless, to doubt) must be intended when such blessing is given now.'

And again —

'Life is such a beautiful thing. So full of love, of possibilities, of blessing; God is so good! — so overflowing with goodness that He cannot help sharing it with the meanest, the weakest, of His creatures. This abounding mercy and goodness surprise the low and empty and thankless heart, and fill it with Itself. It is no longer its own. It cannot remain what it was. It cannot help rising and girding itself for the work given it to do. It is one with God, for God has filled it with Himself.

'And not only with Himself, but in pity for the weakness of this thankless heart, He has given it the human help of which it stood so sorely in need, and for which it prayed — that which it asked for, and none other. This is what makes it tremble with excessive joy. This is what seems too marvellous for belief.'

And again —

'When I think what was before me — what my life seemed likely to be, when this merciful God vouchsafed to visit me with blessing beyond my conception or hope — how helpless

for serving Him — how impossible it seemed
that any way or means should open, or could be
found, whereby such privilege might be mine,
and how! With one on whom the eyes of
England are turned — to whom the dark places
of the earth look with expectation and with
hope — whose eloquence and whose power turn
the desolate places into gardens, and bring light
to those who sit in the shadow of death — and
to live with such a man! To share in such a
work! What am I, and what is my father's
house that such a thing should have happened
to me?'

And once more —

'Is it possible that what is begun in wilful-
ness and self-love is taken into the Divine
Mercy and transmuted into the gold that paves
Its Throne, suffered to co-operate with Its
eternal purpose and will?'

I imagine that something of a chill fell upon
this blissful life somewhat soon. Damerle did
not stay long at Clyston St. Fay. He had
preaching engagements in different parts of the
county which took him away. He wrote in
these days very constantly — letters descriptive

of his aspirations and his work. They were very good letters. I have seen some of them; and Blanche Boteraux read and re-read them till Henri-Frédéric Amiel, even, faded from her mind. But I believe that it is an accepted truth that love is not satisfied with letters, and when Damerle returned to London, after a very hurried visit, life at Clyston St. Fay set in cold and bleak. The London season was drawing to a close. The balconies were gorgeous with brilliant flowers, but there was a languor in the air, and a dusty film upon the brightest colours that showed that the end was not far off.

On a sultry afternoon in this tired season Mr. Damerle turned out of St. James Street into St. James Place and knocked at one of the old-fashioned quiet houses in a remote corner, looking from their back windows upon the Green Park.

All the way, as he had come down, through the streets and squares to the north of Picca-dilly, he had been conscious of the ceaseless roll of carriages — the routine of a London afternoon — every three or four minutes at some door or other the drawing up of a perfectly appointed carriage, the same number of servants at the door, the servant from the carriage with his cards, the mysterious paper indicating some social nicety, then the closed door, the faultless equipage *en route* again, and the indispensable ceremony complete.

All this impressed him, familiar as it was, in the receptivity which was his characteristic and his bane. There was something in this ceaseless flow, this unbroken existence, of a luxury and a system of stately routine that excited his imagination.

Taken in connection with the one theme which, to do him justice, was constantly present in his mind, it seemed to remind him of a time when the preaching of the Cross convinced the proud and noble of the pagan world — kaisers and prætors and delicate women, who could not put their feet to the ground for delicacy, yet, moved by the power of an indwelling Christ, wore sackcloth and dressed the wounds of lepers.

He turned into this remote corner and knocked at the door of a dingy-looking red-brick house. It was opened immediately by three servants.

' Lady Elizabeth Poer ? ' he said.

Though the house was quiet-looking and even dingy on the outside, it was evident, as you went in, that it was no common house.

The square hall which seemed to occupy so much of the front of the house was festooned, on all its walls, with exquisite mouldings of fruit and flowers, and the ceiling was a mass of delicate work. Beyond, the visitor passed through another hall, lighted from above, in which a staircase in bronzed iron and gilt scroll-work led to the upper rooms. All over the walls and ceilings, in faint and delicate colouring, these traceries and wreaths followed him everywhere. At the top of the staircase the passage opened into a small landing, lighted from above, the walls of which were hung with pictures, and then a door was thrown open, and Damerle entered a long, low drawing-room, with a wide bay window, overlooking an expanse of greenwood, with a belt of bright-coloured flowers on the balcony in front. He had seen this room before; but, at the moment he entered it now, something in the form of this window struck him as strangely familiar, and recalled another window, low, and with bay sashes like this, down in remote Devonshire, before which, not so many weeks ago, a girl standing before him, between him and it, he had offered himself and his life.

There was no one in the room. On the walls

and in every corner of it there were dainty works of art—painting, ivories, statuettes, family sketches. portraits, drawings of ancestral homes, all mellowed and toned down into a oneness of perfect tint and thought,—a dream of perfect rest. Some confusion of mind, as of doubt as to where he was,—in which of these two rooms he was about to play a part—seemed to perplex him, as he turned round suddenly, and a lady entered the room.

She was about his own age, and, as nearly as possible, his own height. She was not perhaps exactly beautiful, but she had a grace of manner which is greater than all beauty; yet, as she sat down, after taking his hand, there was, through her grace and urbanity, an expression of reserved power and even aggressiveness which seemed to say, 'Any one who injures or insults me had need beware.'

'I have brought you the papers, about which you were kind enough to take an interest, Lady Elizabeth,' he said; 'the scheme seems to me a good one as far as it goes, but it is a mere drop in the bucket. One is appalled at the hopelessness of the task.'

She took the papers in her hand, but did not look at them; she seemed to be thinking of what he had said.

As she did not speak he went on again; he was always very ready of speech.

'I was thinking of it all, Lady Elizabeth,' he said, 'as I came down Park Lane, and saw all the carriages — the luxury of life. What we want is to divert all this wealth and energy and life, and turn it whither it ought to flow. We want some one in society — some man, or some set of men, men of standing, who entertain, who influence social life.'

'Why cannot you do it?' she said; 'surely no one has more influence than you.'

'I! Lady Elizabeth. what can I do? The men I want to influence never come to church; at least not to my church. If I were to say such things to them, did they come, they would be disgusted and never come again. Even if they were not disgusted, they would pay no heed. They would forget it in a moment. What is wanted is some man of their own order, in their own social life, who will dine with them, talk with them, smoke with them, play billiards, cards, with them — anything to win souls to this work.'

Something in this method of looking at things seemed to accord with her own instinct and taste. She looked at him with an inquiring expectant look, as if waiting to hear more.

The subdued culture, the atmosphere of the room, the delicate scent of ottar from the cabinets, and of the flowers from the window-sills without, the ideas which his own words conveyed, suggested to him, it would seem, a sudden startling thought, which he put from him as the suggestion of a fiend. He rose from his seat.

'It does not do to talk of these things, Lady Elizabeth,' he said. 'I am sorry that I troubled you, but you wished to see the papers.'

She looked at him with extreme surprise, as she too rose from her seat.

'You have not troubled me,' she said.

Nevertheless he left the room, pleading some palpably insufficient excuse.

When she had rung the bell and he was gone, she walked up the long low room and stood for a moment looking over the wide park. A soft wind was blowing from the south-west, making the sky and air almost as clear and pure as over the Surrey downs. Beyond the trees, towards the palace and the distant houses, a faint mist of white smoke rose into the air, becoming fainter and fainter as it rose, and fading by ever more delicate tints of whiteness into the blue, till at last, overhead, the sky seemed pure and clear as over the greenwood of a child's dream. It was a beautiful sight, but she did not see it. It was not that which kept her for a moment at the bay sashes looking out.

It was something that he had said, but much more his sudden rising and going out, that seemed to open to her a future into which she had had no insight hitherto. What this future was we may guess as our fancy prompts us. What is of more importance is that the thought of it, whatever it was, kept her gazing through these old-fashioned window-panes upon the London park. which she never saw, for some time.

Damerle preached that night — it was a Friday — in a South London church — a church that stood upon the verge of respectability, and included among its congregation the well-to-do and the poor. It was a fine old church, with several aisles and lines of pillars and lofty roofs. Although it was a week-day night, yet the fame of the great preacher drew a very fair congregation, and the vast church did not look bare or unfilled. All through the service people were coming in, many in working-clothes, and when

Damerle went into the pulpit he saw little else than a sea of eager white faces turned to his.

He preached from two texts, a habit of his; in the selection of which he was often very happy. This evening his texts were: 'Lead us not into temptation,' and 'The devil entered into Judas Iscariot.'

'"Lead us not into temptation." These words spoken — no, I am wrong — not spoken merely, but introduced into that short but all-sufficient rule and method by which He taught His chosen and beloved to approach the Infinite Father — *lead* us not into temptation! spoken by Him who needed not that any should teach Him, for He knew all men; nay, not only all men, but God Himself; it must mean very much, such words as these: "*Lead* us not into temptation"; not only suffer us not to fall into temptation, but do not Thyself lead us into it; the Greek is awfully strong — do not Thou carry us into, urge us into temptation! Not alone in unguarded moments — though all moments are unguarded before the supreme enemy of souls, — but while engaged in God's work, or what we fondly dream is God's work, in hours when everything is bright around us; the clearness of thought, the perfection of taste, the luxury of life, the pure smile of good women, inspiring and urging to a higher, to a more devoted walk; when the soul is lulled into a fond conviction that here at least there can be no need of suspicion, of cause for fear. Then — then more than ever — let us pray, *Lead* us not into temptation, O God! For then. suspicionless and void of fear — all nature, men and angels, God Himself smiling upon us — are we ensnared by the devil and taken captive by him at his will; and there are men who tell us, smiling, that there is no such thing as evil at all!

'And the devil entered into Judas Iscariot, where? At the Paschal supper and table of the Lord! Oh. lead us; leave us not in temptation, most merciful God!'

When Damerle came into the vestry, following the other clergy. he was deathly pale. They offered him a glass of water.

'You are tired, Mr. Damerle.' said the Rector of the parish. 'It must take it out of you, preaching these great sermons day after day. We are very much obliged to you, I am sure.'

'Yes,' said Damerle. 'you are right. It takes it out of me very much indeed.'

VIII

On a propitious day of summer, if you stand on some extreme verge of Exmoor, if we may call that Exmoor which extends as far as West Down above Ilfracombe, and see the coast of North Devon, westward by Bull Light, and Morthoe, and Clovelly, and Hartland Point, with the dazzling flashing channel, and Lundy Island, with its long dark outline, to the right, and overhead a royal oriflamme of sky and mystic tracery of cloud pencilling, you will see something which, I hope, for your sake, you will not soon forget. It was perhaps a month, or maybe two — time passes so fast — after Mr. Damerle had preached that sermon in South London, that he stood by Blanche Boteraux on this very spot. They had driven some dozen miles from Clyston St. Fay to a little inn where the horses were put up, and Damerle and Blanche ascended the moor alone. Afterwards Blanche remembered the day, for there were certain words spoken by Damerle, certain indications of tendency, which she recalled in after-days.

The little inn lay in a lovely valley surrounded by woods of oak and larches and fir, and long rows of stately elms, stretching across the meadows. There was a church with a massive tower with buttresses, and with oaken roofs, and wooden seats, three centuries old, carved at the ends, with emblems of the Passion, and with initials indicating departed kings and queens, both Anglican and Romanist.

They went up a winding lane, where the wild roses and woodbine hung, and the great fronds of hart's-tongue and polypodium stretched across the narrow path.

From the earliest dawn of spring, when the gorse and the primroses, like sunlight and moonlight, combine to welcome the blue sky above, to the latest day of autumn, these lanes are perhaps the most perfect places upon this earth; yet Damerle and Blanche walked up them with scarcely a word or thought of their beauty.

They went up on to the moor. It was a soft clear summer day. The colouring which the spring had brought upon the land was over, and, in its place, a faded green made the most perfect foreground and setting for the long delicate coast-line of sea and sky, drawn out along the horizon in infinite shadings of tint and tracing up into the summer blue above. A line of marvellously slight and dazzling whiteness marked the sea-foam breaking along the coast, and above this shades of greens and browns of indescribable beauty led the eye up to the shadowed blues and whites of the summer sky and cloud. Beyond the white line the opal tints of blue and gold, as the sea-waves flashed up against the sunlight, spread themselves over the wide channel almost beyond the reach of sight. The shores and coves of the old historic seamen and harbour towns lay silent beneath the sunlight and the summer sky, a vast temple of the God of Hosts, within which the sense shrank, bewildered at the conception at the same moment of the littleness and the greatness of man, the sole occupant and worshipper in this boundless temple, the story of whose existence and struggle is the sole service and anthem ever heard beneath its dome.

The two stood for some time in silence, looking at this marvellous sight. Then Blanche said—

'I suppose it is very beautiful, but I don't

care for it. It is always the case with me. I have seen the Alps from the Jura; I have seen the lake from the gardens and terraces of Bellagio, which they say is the most beautiful view in the world, but none of these speak to me. I always want to get at mankind, at human nature, to help the great human needs. God never seems to speak to me in such scenes as these.'

'Jacobi,' said Damerle, — 'Jacobi, who was a great German thinker, says "Nature conceals God, man reveals Him." Still, I am not a Manichean. I think that Nature has its uses. You yourself, when you are older and have felt more of the storm and stress of life, will probably find such a scene as this consoling — invigorating. Work among the poor and needy is very wearing; especially if you are poor yourself.'

'Poor!' said Blanche with a startled look; 'I thought that it was to the poor that we were sent, and that "the Lord was poor."'

'Yes, the Lord was poor,' replied Damerle, with some slight touch of irritation in his tone; 'but the Lord had resources which we have not. To really help the poor, you must be rich. One rich man can do more good than all the sermons

in the world, not only by what he may give,
but in influencing other rich people; and to
influence rich people, especially in London, you
must yourself be rich.'

'But you are so much sought after,' she said;
'people flock so much to your preaching. Surely
you will be able to influence the rich.'

'Yes,' he said; 'I hope to. I am not without
hopes of getting one of the great West End
churches near Hyde Park. I have applied for
it. The position and influence are very great.
The income is large.'

'And shall we go there?' she said, still more
aghast. It was certainly very different from the
home and the life of which she had dreamed — a
home in poverty-haunted districts of London,
where, blessing, and being sanctified by such
blessing, life would become a holy and immortal
thing.

Of poverty, as it might affect herself, she had
absolutely no conception. From her birth everything that was desirable, both for culture and
necessities, had been hers, as it seemed, as a
matter of course. She regarded poverty somewhat as a French princess of the last century,
who was *dévote*, might have thought of some
quiet and *négligé* but very elegant morning dress,

suitable to wear in retreat. It should be said for her that, had she known more of its stern reality, her decision, I believe, would have been much the same.

'Well,' she said gently. — she was very gentle with him — 'if you wish for it, I hope that you will get it; but it is not what I thought. What is it that Canon Liddon said about being strangled by a silken thread in luxurious drawing-rooms?'

He made no answer to this home-thrust, and they went on, hand in hand as it were, through this paradise of God's creation that lay around them on every side.

Mr. Damerle returned to London, but he did not go alone. The Rector and Blanche accompanied him. They went to a relative of Dr. Boteraux, a great lady in Eaton Square. The London season, indeed, had long been over, and the Boterauxs do not seem to have partaken of such diversions even as remained. Damerle carried them off every morning to the east and north of London, where the Rector was introduced to scenes with which he was not familiar, and in which he was not seen to advantage. In the life of such a man one such change as that from the common room of St. Nodimus to a little village in North Devon, was as much as could reasonably be expected to be accomplished with any approach to success. The Boterauxs did not stay very long in London, and there is no reason to suppose that they were introduced to, or even knew of, the existence of Lady Elizabeth Poer.

But to Blanche Boteraux these few days were a revelation of a clearer vision and insight, and of a widened experience and hope. It was to her young life, as it were, a raising of the painted drop-scene, so that the drama of life might be revealed in all its acts and scenes. It seemed to her that she had never lived before. In the variety of that strange life, hitherto only dimly guessed at, which crossed her path in those few hours, in its terrible pathos, in its humour, in the transient flashes of sunlight that shone across it, she seemed to see the inexhaustible interests and blessing of a work that the coming years were bringing to her; and by her side — the herald and master spirit of this work — was he to whom she had given herself, to whom she had pledged herself, and who was pledged to her. It does not require much effort of the imagination to realise, at least in some degree, what a prospect of immortal life and action was opening to her heart. I find one passage in her diary.

written about this time, which seems to have been amplified from Amiel. Much of it is her own.

'The best path through life is the high road, which initiates at the right moment into all experience. The high road is where common life most abounds, — most of the suffering, all the interest of life, is there. What is common is at once most safe, most honest, and most wholesome. Cross roads may tempt us by their loveliness, by the stillness and refinement and culture of their retired recesses and walks, but the temptation is towards self and self-seeking, and we are likely to regret the choice. It is only where a common want leads to a common end that the faithful servant of God and of the race is found.'

Not very long after their return from London George Falaise turned up at Clyston St. Fay at the end of the Long Vacation. He was not much altered. When a boy develops as early as he had done, a term or two at college does not make much difference in him; but he was older, and he seemed to act under certain restraint, which contrasted unpleasantly with his previous boyish unembarrassment. The Rector was always delighted to see him, and prophesied great things relating to his degree. It did not seem at first very clear why he came, for there was no shooting, and he had not been expected so soon; but Blanche was afraid that she divined the reason, and it soon proved that she was right.

They were sitting one afternoon upon the garden-seat, outside the drawing-room window, where he had sat on that morning after his first arrival, so long ago, as it seemed, now.

It was the full blaze of the late summer now. Through the long aftermath, and down the glades and pathways of the wood, a distinct and perceptible stillness, that might be felt, pressed itself upon the sense.

It was this moment of supreme stillness and colour and this place, propitious to him in the past, which George Falaise chose in which to say his say.

'So, I suppose, you are going to marry this man, Blanche,' he said.

'If you mean Mr. Damerle,' she said, rather coldly, 'I believe I am.'

'Well,' he said, 'I will not say any harm of a fellow, but you will make a great mistake if you do.   You had much better marry me.'

'But I can't, George,' she said, almost laughing; 'I am engaged to Mr. Damerle.'

'Well,' he said, 'it's a shame — a cruel shame. You are the only girl I want.   I am premier-viscount of England — we might have been earls or anything — and there are lots of money; I suppose there are any number of girls I could have, but I don't want them.   I want you.   I may be a fool, but I know a good thing when I see it.   I know a good woman when I see her, and I will have her and none other; and I asked you first,' he added, in a deeply injured tone, almost like that of a child who is about to cry.

'You make a great mistake when you speak like that,' she said. 'I am not good. It would be a fatal thing for you to marry me.'

He sat for a minute or two silent, apparently commanding himself, then he got up from his seat.

'Well,' he said, standing before her, 'I said I would not say anything against Damerle to you; that wouldn't be fair. I hope he will make you as good a husband as I should have wished to do.'

There was something in his manner and in his restraint of expression that struck her. She had a woman's instinct, clear and true enough to tell her that he loved her with a passion which she had not felt in another, and his self-command and reserve inspired her with a cordial respect. She showed it in her look and tone.

'Whoever you marry, George,' she said, 'will be a happy girl. You will soon forget me.'

'No,' he said, 'I shan't;' and he sat down by her side again. 'Do you know how we got our name? We are called Falaise from the beating of the sea upon a stony beach. The first thing that I remember at all, and the only thing that I remember of my father, was his telling me that. I was a very little boy — a baby indeed — and they came to me one day and told me that I must be very good and come and see my father, who was going away for a very long time. And they took me into a great room, where he lay in a bed, and my mother was there. And he lay very still and looked at me for a long time with his hand upon my arm; and he said, " My boy, do you know how you got your name? You are called Falaise from the beating of the sea upon the stony beach. And do you know what your motto is? — 'Je fais fort et je falaise'; and it means, 'I make myself strong, and I persist.'" Of course I did not understand what he said, and I don't suppose that I heard the words, for he spoke very low, but I remember how he looked very well; and my mother wrote it down, and I have it in a locket — here.'

She was deeply moved. She looked at him with still kindlier eyes.

' Whoever you marry, George,' she said again, 'will be a happy girl.'

It is easy to say these things, and they mean very little after all.

George Falaise did not stay long at Clyston St. Fay. He was going back to Oxford at once. Damerle wrote in one of his weekly letters that he had missed the living near Hyde Park. He had been one of the two finally selected by the trustees, but the other man had been chosen. He wrote somewhat bitterly about it. He had several other livings offered him, but they were not such as he felt inclined to accept. He regretted the disappointment the more because it condemned him to a longer delay in consummating his highest hopes.

So the months drew on — the slow, quiet, wearisome months at Clyston St. Fay. There are long hours and days and weeks in the country in summer and autumn, heavy with the scent of lilies, soft with the flakes of scattered petal and blossom, of rose-leaves, and hydrangea flowers, and strewn jessamine — a fairy carpet that makes the garden-path soft beneath the tread. Life might seem as delicious at such moments as was that wasted in the enchanted castles and gardens of romance, but it does not satisfy the young enthusiastic heart, thirsting for activity in beneficent work. During these long and sultry hours almost the sole incident in Blanche Boteraux's life, the only mental and spiritual sustenance apart from some of her books, was the weekly letter from London. I have said that these were good letters. I may say more: I may say that no girl could conceive a method of life, a devotion of aim, higher than these letters revealed.

The summer and the autumn passed away. Damerle wrote to say that he could not come down to Devonshire for Christmas, but that he would try to come for the New Year. George Falaise would come down for Christmas, and stay till the Lent term began. A very good report of George reached the Rector from his old friends at St. Nod's. When he came down on Christmas Eve, and she saw him in the drawing-room as she came in before dinner, Blanche thought that he was changed — much changed in the last few months. He seemed older, quieter. He never was noisy; but he seemed within the last few months to have lost his boyish springiness, and to have developed an air of lassitude and of extreme distinction, which she was not sure that she liked. She felt what might seem an inconsistent interest and proprietorship in his well-doing and behaviour. As a sister, as a mother even, if he would have had it, there was no perfection of sympathy she would not have given him.

The room was dimly lighted by a shaded lamp; candles in branched sockets about the walls would be lighted after dinner. It was necessary to study economy at Clyston St. Fay.

'Good evening,' she said, holding out her hand, as she came in; 'I hope you have had a pleasant journey.'

As she came up softly in the shaded light over the worn old Turkey carpet, she looked to George Falaise like an angel in white llama, with pink camellias in her dress.

He took her hand, and held it for a second or two, but he did not speak.

She was perfectly self-possessed, and stood looking at him with a friendly, even affectionate gaze.

'You look older than you did in the summer,' she said.

It was a strange contrast from that first meeting in that very room, just over two years ago, when he did all the talking, and she was disdainful and angry at the sight of him. Now he seemed to be tongue-tied and abashed, and she, serene in the possession of so glorious a present and so priceless a future, was able, without effort and without nervousness, to look down upon this brilliant, beautiful, but, she felt somehow. unhappy and disappointed boy — no, he was no longer a boy — from a pinnacle of disinterested pity and interest.

Still he did not speak. They stood looking into the fire for some moments.

At last he drew himself up. with the movement of a man who had conquered, with no small effort, the inclination to say something else.

· Yes, I have had a very pleasant journey, for I was thinking all the way that I should see Dr. Boteraux and you again.'

' Have you been quite well?' she said, looking at him full in the eyes.

It is needless to describe the effect that her look, her personality, her friendliness. had upon him; yet he did not falter nor vary from his set purpose at all.

' Well?' he said, with something of his old boyish smile; 'oh yes, quite well, thank you. Why?'

' You look changed — older, somehow,' she said; and she too this time dropped her eyes, and stood silently looking into the fire.

At this moment, fortunately, who knows? the Doctor came into the room.

' Ah! my dear boy,' he said; 'delighted to

see you. Well, what is it to be? First in
" greats " ? '

'Oh no, sir; I don't think I shall be in the
first at all.'

The Friday before the first Sunday in the
New Year, Damerle came down. He too was
altered. He seemed more excited and nervous.
He talked incessantly — very brilliantly, no
doubt, but too much. The contrast between
the two men was more marked than ever, now
that in age and outward appearance they were
more equal, and to a disinterested observer the
change was altogether in favour of George Falaise. He seemed to consider himself merely
the guest of the Rector. He addressed himself
to him at meals. He left the talking entirely
to Damerle. He avoided the society both of
him and of Blanche. The Rector was much
quieter than formerly. He too seemed aged
and tired.

On the first Sunday in the year, at the morning service, Damerle preached. It was without
doubt a great sermon, and it made a considerable
impression even on the fastidious congregation
of Clyston St. Fay.

'The dawn had broke that day over the bare

branches of the apple trees, and the withered oak woods, full of hope and healing, till some faint reflection of its glory had reached even the pallid western sky, and the dun moor, and the western sea — the sea of expectance, and of adventure, and of wealth. But another day had dawned on every one of us — the first day of another movement on life's dial — another of those awful pausings in life's struggle which are given us, in mercy, to warn us as we pass.

'In the solemn sunrise of another year every one of us is standing at gaze on the waste forward pathways of his life. A year we call it, and prate of days and hours, and scientific divisions, and moments of time; but in truth it is a year, the moments of which are men's passionate and wilful actions, and each chiming of a passing hour, to which perchance we pay no heed, is in truth the proclamation of doom that awaits some *one* unready or ungracious at life's feast.

'As I looked upon the dawn this morning there seemed to me angelic stairways and paths traced upon the sky. As we look upon the sea are there not mystic pathways traced there also? To what bourne? to what haven? will these untried, yet beaten, ways lead each of us?

What is the doom that will await us in the coming hours? Is there in any of us the heart of unbelief that trembles at his own future — that sees before him, by the light of that, as yet, not quite extinguished conscience, some possibilities that make him cry, " Is thy servant a dog, that he should do this thing? that he should do this wickedness and live?" Oh, if there be any one here present — eh! if it were the preacher himself, who sees anything before him that looks like this, I beg of him, by the mercies of God, by the love that has followed him from a child, to turn whilst there is yet time.'

The sermon had an immense effect. Farmer Wray of the Fen Cannons went so far as seriously to consider, as he went home, whether his neighbour Lob of Filbeigh was actually meditating passing off another broken-winded gelding at Barnstaple Fair.

They were rather quiet at lunch at the rectory. The Rector was much more silent than formerly, and none of the others seemed to have anything to say. After lunch, the weather being very mild for the season, the three younger people strolled out on to the grassy verge between the deer paddock and the bay-window of the drawing-room, and

Damerle accepted a cigar that George Falaise offered him.

Blanche was standing as though she were looking across the paddock, in the centre of which the deer were feeding, but she did not see them. She was looking into a beatific sky beyond a waste of mystic sea.

Suddenly Damerle began to speak. He seemed to be the subject of some impelling power, in the guidance of an insight greater than his own, that compelled him to speak in spite of himself, to excuse and to defend where, seemingly, there was no need.

'All the time I was preaching this morning,' he said, 'I had a sense of fate, of the unalterable future which none can avoid. There are times when the coils of circumstance are so wound about a man, and his own personality is so in accord with the persuasive drawing of these coils, that his case is hopeless and foredoomed. I fancy that I was preaching to myself, and not to you.'

George Falaise took his cigar from his mouth. 'Is there not,' he said slowly — he always spoke slowly now — 'is there not a line of Tenny-son's —

'"Man is man and master of his fate"?'

'And there is prayer to God,' said Blanche.

> ' "There is a little rift within the lute,
>   Which by and by will make the music mute," '

Damerle said; 'the hope and guard of his existence is taken from him, for the very form and nature of his being is undermined and fractured by a predetermined fate.'

'Oh, do not say that!' she said; 'I do not like it. Let us walk a little way.'

He threw away his half-finished cigar, and placed himself by her side, and they walked up the woodland path that wound round the paddock. George Falaise stood looking at them for a moment as they moved up the path — but only for a moment. Then he turned away and moved towards the seat before the bay-window of the drawing-room — the same seat on which he had sat that first morning when Blanche had come out to him. There he sat down to finish his cigar.

The winter sun, setting behind the oak woods on the other side of the paddock, cast a kind of false and cold halo over the place where he sat and over the front of the house. He felt deserted and neglected. He hated this man. The cold winter sky, clear and soft and delicate though it was, out of the cloud tissues of which happy men might weave fairy-coloured wreaths, seemed to him dun and chill. The stillness was so profound that the deer, leaving their fodder, strayed up towards the house with wistful. pathetic eyes and questing looks, and quiet pausings now and then, rather lured on than disturbed by his motionless figure. But. in the chill and gloom of desertion and disappointment, in response to something within himself, he seemed to hear an answering voice assuring him that the words of the great poet he had quoted were indeed no idle words. Nevertheless, he hated this man.

For about a quarter of an hour perhaps he had sat there. The rhythm of the breeze through the surrounding woods soothed him as did the narcotic influence of his cigar, when the setting sun, just sinking behind the woods. cast a sudden glow of dying brilliancy over the place, and above, over his head, a golden haze of glory spread itself, beneath the rain-clouds and the deep winter sky. He looked up suddenly, and they were coming back. He rose, threw away the end of his cigar, and went towards them.

Damerle evidently had been talking well. Whatever he was he was no hypocrite. Whatever he felt, for the moment, he really felt. The climate, physical and mental, of Clyston St. Fay affected him, with an intensity which it would not have exerted upon another man, less easily affected in other ways. George Falaise even, who felt himself, so to speak, a stranger and a pilgrim everywhere else; to whom this silent village, this home where Blanche lived, was the only spot upon earth, so far as he knew the earth, where he seemed really to breathe — even he did not feel this excited revulsion and contrast of feeling and of enthusiasm. Damerle had been speaking of high and sacred things and of the work which lay before them, for the girl's face was flushed, and her whole being and nature seemed instinct with a strange happiness and beauty which was not of earth. Never before, at any time, and most surely never afterwards, did George Falaise see her look like that, — the departing flash of sunset around her, the set purpose of devotion, the glory of unselfish love, the beauty which God gave to woman, all around her for a moment as they came up the path.

The angry, disappointed, perturbed spirit left him at this sight. All self-seeking, all self even, was lost in delight. He felt, in spite of himself, a supreme stillness and calm, a sense of result, of something, long wished for, being gained. It is a great mystery why such things are; but to him, to whom so much had been given, had been

added also the priceless gift of unselfish love.
To what issue can love tend but to the happiness
of the loved? The perfect vision that awaits
love must surely be this. At this happy moment, as it seems to me, many of us might well
envy him; yet at that moment, the one thing
in the wide universe that was denied him was
the one thing upon which his heart was set.

As they came up the path the sunset glow
faded from the sky above, and what a moment
before had been a glory of yellow light was now
gray and dark. They went back into the house.

They were all dispersed soon after this.
Damerle went back to London, George to Oxford, Blanche went to visit a clergyman's family
whom she knew at Bridgetown. She wanted to
see as much as she could of church life in towns,
but she had not the heart to stay long away from
her father, who seemed to fail and age so much.
When she came back to Clyston St. Fay, the
place seemed very quiet and dull. Bridgetown
is not a gay place, nor would you instinctively
look to it as affording a lively scene of action in
any sphere of human interest, but it was life and
activity itself compared with Clyston St. Fay.
As the months went on — the silent uneventful
life — broken only by the Sundays, through the

long slow course of which Blanche lived, as it were, only upon the beating of her heart — Damerle did not write so regularly as before, and at last did not write at all. Blanche made every allowance for him, and wrote herself far oftener than he deserved; but she could not keep on writing when no answers came, when, morning after morning, the wished-for letter was not there.

George Falaise wrote frequently, always to Dr. Boteraux. He was not happy about his degree. He had been in the first class in 'Mods.,' but he did not believe that he should be in the first *in literis Humanoribus*. However, when the lists came out, there it was; quite certainly 'Viscount Falaise.' The Rector was very pleased. 'Je fais fort et je falaise,' he said.

I have been turning over these old lists all the evening, trying to picture to myself those old days, to revive once again those old efforts and hopes. What realities exist somewhere, or did exist, about every name! What expectations, what fond desires, how much love! What does it matter now? I had almost thought. I should have been wrong. It matters very much. The place of every name has a meaning, and a joy or sting, somewhere, in some heart, even now.

X

So the summer and the autumn passed away.
It is the custom of the gentry of Devon, of those
of them at least who live within possible distance, to visit Minsterley, the Cathedral city, on
one or two days of the week. It is a survival
of that delightful time when the county town
was the resort of the people of the county during
the winter, when the stately, red-brick houses,
clustered round the Cathedral or the Castle, were
the home of culture and refinement during the
winter months, in numberless centres of county
life throughout the land. In the faint reflex of
this custom at Minsterley there was the Club,
and there was shopping, and there was the meeting of each other in the street, that made the
visit pleasant. Dr. Boteraux was frequently
there on a Thursday. He was rarely able to
persuade his daughter to accompany him. She
disliked the crowded High Street, the gay

158

dresses of the ladies, the shopping, and the pleasant. careless, not very intellectual talk. Even the subdued, restful Minster interior, with its perfect harmony of soft colour, and the sweet singing of its choir — a service unsurpassed, I might say unequalled, in England — did not seem to attract her. The pleasant things of life, even when sanctified, were not to her mind. She had a longing, or thought that she had, for the unattractive and distasteful — a genius for martyrdom, some would have called it. only it was not martyrdom to her. I have thought often with a delighted admiration how completely in the after time she mastered this tendency, when she felt it her duty so to do.

That Thursday morning at breakfast there was still no letter. The letters came in early at Clyston St. Fay, being dropped at the nearest station. and brought over by a boy before breakfast. The Rector was looking at his daughter now and again anxiously over his plate. It was not the first morning that he had done this.

'This mullet is really very good, my dear.' he said at last; 'I wish you would take some. It comes from Plymouth. Binns has some personal friend there who gets it for him. Otherwise, it all goes up to London. It is a singular result of civilisation that no fish is procurable at the seaside nowadays. I am told that Birmingham, the very centre of England, is the best supplied place for fish in the country, and that all the fish for the seaside watering-places is sent from Birmingham. They can't get fish at Aberystwith, say, till the train comes in from Birmingham. Think of that!'

Blanche took a little of the mullet mechanically, and her father kept prattling on with a kind of despair in his tone.

'I suppose you won't come into Minsterley to-day, my dear,' he said; 'I think it would do you good.'

He went to Minsterley alone, and on the sunny afternoon of that day he was strolling down the High Street, looking into the old-book shops, and exchanging a passing word, now with a beautifully-dressed lady, now with a genial but dignified west country squire. Somewhere about the Guildhall he came upon a clergyman whom he only slightly knew, who, somewhat to Dr. Boteraux's surprise, instead of merely bowing and passing on, stopped and shook hands. Then he turned and seemed inclined to walk with the Rector. He made some passing remarks upon the weather and upon the last apple crop, remarked that he had been to London; but still he did not go away. He was so evidently embarrassed that the Rector felt bound to help him.

'I never can get to London,' he said; 'not that I want to go.'

'Dr. Boteraux,' said the other, making a desperate rush at something which he hesitated, and yet wished, to say,—'Dr. Boteraux, I heard something, when in London, that surprised me very much, and which I can hardly believe, though I heard it from a most trustworthy source. I am not sure whether I ought to tell you or not; but meeting you so suddenly and unexpectedly — for I am very seldom in Minsterley — something comes into my mind that urges me to tell it to you, although I hesitate very much. It is no secret, I believe, that your daughter is engaged to Paul Damerle, the great preacher. Now I heard more than once in London, and it was there spoken of as certain, that he is going to marry — it was told me very soon —another woman, a lady of rank and fortune. Forgive me if I have done wrong in speaking to you.'

Dr. Boteraux was a man of nerve, and a gentleman of the old school; he succeeded in suppressing any outward sign of emotion; but it was by an effort that cost him very dear. He was old, and the last few months had broken and aged him very much. Had he received the information anywhere but on the public street, it is probable that he would have broken down.

'I thank you very much, sir,' he said slowly, and with very apparent effort, 'for not keeping back this distressing news from me. It distresses me very much, as you may suppose; but I cannot say that it comes upon me altogether unprepared. I thank you very much.'

The other looked at him with some anxiety; but it was so evident that he wished to be left alone that there was nothing to be done but to leave him.

'I hope it is not true. Dr. Boteraux,' he said feebly; 'but I fear that it is. I cannot say,' he added, with a desperate attempt at concluding the interview with some appearance of cheerfulness, — 'I cannot say that I have so much admiration for great preachers as some have; probably because I am not one myself. Good-bye.'

'Good-bye, and thank you.'

Dr. Boteraux turned round the moment that the other had moved off, and slowly made his way through the crowded street. without speaking or seeing any one until he reached the station. He had to wait some time for his train. He went into the refreshment room and had a glass of brandy and water, then he sat for the remainder of the time in a dark corner of the waiting-room until the train came up.

'I am a dead man,' he said to himself over and over again. 'I shall never get over this. Blanche! Blanche!'

All the way home to the roadside station, some three miles from Clyston St. Fay, he was wondering what he must do: whether he must tell his daughter or not? Fortunately, there was no one in the carriage whom he knew. The train was an earlier one than that mostly used by the gentry of his part of the county. His carriage met him at the station, but before he entered it he had made up his mind that he could not tell her, at any rate not that night. It would be better to wait for confirmation. But he could not conceal from his daughter that he was tired.

'It is too much for you going to Minsterley in the day, father,' she said; 'I am afraid that you will have to give it up.'

'I am afraid I shall, my dear.'

But at dinner he recovered himself a little,

and exerted himself gallantly to talk and to
entertain his daughter. He told her everything
that he could remember of what the ladies had
said to him, of the appearance of the shops, of an
old book that had attracted him, of the lectures
that were announced, of the gossip about the
vacant canonry. She was struck with his gentle
and benign manner—his more than usual kindli-
ness. Her heart was drawn to her father more
than it had ever been; she seemed to see in him
something which she had never seen before. It
was his habit to retire to his study immediately
after dinner, and to come into the drawing-room
afterwards for a cup of tea, but he did not
leave his daughter that night. He stayed in
the drawing-room with her till tea was brought
in, talking pleasantly to the end; then he ex-
cused himself on the plea of fatigue and went
to bed. Whether he slept at all that night I
cannot say.

How he passed the next two or three days he
probably could hardly have told; but he had not
long to wait. He wrote more than one letter
to friends in London, but he tore them up. It
seemed like inviting the lightning to strike his
home. Whether he acted wisely or not it
would be difficult to decide. Probably it did not

matter very much what he did. The end was near.

One morning, a little less than a week after his visit to Minsterley, the Doctor was up early — he could not sleep much in those days — the sweet summer air lured him into the garden. The fresh summer breeze sweeping over the wide woods and earth and sky cheered and invigorated the old man. He lingered, as if moved by some strange instinct, by some intimation that these peaceful moments were the last he would enjoy. After a time he went back into the house; there, on the white cloth of the breakfast-table, lay a letter — the long wished-for letter there at last.

He stood with his back to the window, by which he had entered the room, looking at this letter. 'Should he burn it? there was yet time.' There was a small, comfortable fire upon the hearth, for the rooms were apt to feel chilly in the mornings. For a moment, perhaps, the inevitable fate might be delayed — the irresistible grappled with, perhaps, who knows? slain. But the boy knew that he had brought the letter; the servants had seen it; and. more than all, he felt that the blow that had been struck must fall some time, however fond love might throw itself fruitlessly in the way. He hesitated, and after some minutes his daughter came into the room.

Poor old man! In this commonplace country dining-room, with the old portraits of his mother as a young bride, and of his father in a yeomanry dress, very stiff about the neck, and the worn hearthrug upon which he stood, and the white tablecloth, and the letter, and this striking-looking girl coming in in her simple morning dress, fresh with the freshness of the dawn, there is something, incongruous as it may seem, that recalls to me the old classic stage, and those terrors and sufferings that were borne alike by the father and the child. He saw the speaking light that came into her eyes, he saw the flush of long-deferred delight upon her face, as she saw the letter upon the white cloth. Poor old man!

She took up the letter, opened it and began to read. For a second or two her face kept the look of delight and hope. then it suddenly paled, and the whole figure shrank and faded, so to speak. into something strange to the sight, and she turned to her father, as she had never turned before, with a kind of groping. blind helplessness which was beyond all strength of endurance for a man to be compelled to see.

'I — don't understand this — father — what does it mean?'

And she held the letter out for him to read.

It was a poor letter. The greatest genius upon earth would have found it difficult to write a good letter so as to tell what Damerle had to tell, and Damerle was not, by any means, the greatest genius upon earth. It said that the writer had, after very great distress of mind, arrived at the conclusion that it would be useless and wrong, considering the circumstances in which they were placed, to encourage her, any longer, to unite her fate to his. He had not succeeded in obtaining a living of sufficient amount to enable him, not only to maintain a wife so as he felt himself bound to do, but also, what was perhaps even more important, to carry on and to promote the work that was so dear to both of them. Under these circumstances he had, most slowly and reluctantly, and after very earnest consideration, decided that it would be for the happiness of both that their engagement should be at an end. Though it was an unspeakably painful thing to have to do, it might be as well, the letter said, honestly to confess that he was on the point of forming a matrimonial connection with a Christian lady of rank.

It may seem to some inconceivable that a man should write such words as these; but it is to be remarked that when you have committed an action of unspeakable meanness there is not much choice of language left to you. It is probably the best way, if there can be a better or a worse in such a case, to state the shameful fact in the baldest way. When the deed is once committed the rest signifies but little. Damerle was clever enough to feel this, and he probably consoled himself with the thought that Blanche's affection had been given more to his personality than to his person, and that, when the idol was shattered, she would soon cease to think of the discredited shrine. There was a certain tone in his letter, even, which seemed to show that he pitied himself, as the most injured party, in having such a very unpleasant duty put upon him. The power of the human heart in the direction of self-deception is practically unlimited.

Dr. Boteraux took the letter into his shaking hand and made a feint of reading it, but he did not see a word.

'I do not understand it, father; what does it mean?'

He made a little speech which he had conned over continually during the last three days.

'It means, my dear, that you have now no one to love but me.'

She looked at him again with that terrible look, which was so insupportable to bear — a vague, purposeless, inconsequent look.

'I do not understand. What does it mean?'

Then she almost snatched the letter from his hand, with an impatient gesture, and with it still in her hand, she went out through the open window, crossed the grass. and sat down upon the seat outside the bay-window of the drawing-room, where others had sat before. The Rector followed her to the corner of the house and stood for a moment and watched. She read the letter all through steadily once, then she turned it over and began again — this she did three or four times. It became too terrible to be borne. He went out upon the grass.

She looked up as he came near and held out the letter.

'What does it mean?' she said again. 'I don't understand it. What does it mean?'

And in her look, and in her gesture, there was still that inconsequent, meaningless, almost imbecile gaze.

He sat down on the seat beside her, and

put his arm around her. He spoke as in a kind of dream, so entirely did the words seem to be put into his mouth.

'It means, my dear, that there is nothing in the world except Love. It means that everything that is not Love is but the shadow and the negation of what *is*. Love is all; that is what it means;' and he held her fast in his grasp.

The superb paradox and hyperbole seemed to force itself through her stunned sense. Some kind of light and comprehension came into her dazed and blank eyes. She rested her head upon his shoulder.

Had he followed his first instinct and burnt this terrible letter, the consequences would have been much the same. There were no prayers that morning at Clyston St. Fay Rectory, there was no breakfast eaten; but even before that morning that letter had been foreseen; almost before the Rector had heard the tidings in Minsterley, everything that had happened — that Damerle had married, or was about to marry, a Lady Elizabeth Poer — had been known throughout the whole country-side.

By lunch-time things had, to outward seem-ing, resumed their wonted course. 'Luncheon, sir,' said Mr. Binns, in a perfectly unaltered voice, opening the door of the study where the Rector sat. Hearts must be broken, but the life of the world must go on. The milk-man will still come, early in the morning, and it is as well that he should.

Two days, each of twenty-four slowly dragging sleepless hours, passed away, and it was Sunday, the first Sunday in the month.

There was always a communion at Clyston St. Fay on the first Sunday in the month. There were not many communicants, as a rule, but there was a solemn hush and stillness in the air, and over the whole parish, at that particular moment, as though something mysterious and beyond the common was taking place. This was especially the case on fine summer Sundays, after the first service was over when, on ordinary days, boys and young men lingered about the church-yard and the village road. On these first Sundays of the month no one was to be seen. At such times there was a stillness and pause, during which Nature herself seemed to hold her breath, and the yew trees, and the apple orchards, and the rows of stately elms, lay passive and silent in the sunlight glow, and seemed to own and to proclaim a Presence.

which was of earth and yet divine, to await the tread of the feet of heavenly messengers, the rustle of angelic wings, the gift of heavenly food that nourishes all conditions and ranks alike.

There was a larger congregation than was usually the case on this particular Sunday, many people from the neighbouring parishes coming in.

The Rector preached a well-known sermon. 'The Unrelenting Steward, or the Forgiveness of Wrongs.'

It was a favourite sermon, but not of equal popularity with 'The Ungrateful Son.' It was listened to, to-day, with an unusual relish. A sense of personal interest, of something real and vital, that entered into the life of each and every one, seemed to pervade the church. The well-remembered, sonorous sentence that concluded the sermon was uttered, and the congregation waited for the ascription, that they might rise in their seats, but it did not come. There was a pause, during which the Rector seemed bracing himself to an unusual effort, then he went on again, speaking now without note or book.

'I have not done. There is something more which I have to say. An event has occurred here, where so few events occur, which is by this time known to you all.'

It would take a very great preacher—I doubt whether there is one now living in England who, in the ordinary course of his calling, could do it —to produce such a hush as followed upon these words.

The Rector went on, it is possible somewhat incoherently—

'A stunning blow, dealt at that part where I am most vulnerable, of which you are all thinking, has caused in your hearts, always so kindly affectioned to me and mine, indignation and grief. From the depth of my heart, the heart of a stricken man, I thank you for this last token of your affection and regard. But I have preached to you now for a lengthened time —long. that is, in relation to the short space given us to work in here—of many high and difficult things. I have enforced, as was my duty, many duties upon you; woe be to me if, when my turn comes, I do not, at least, recognise my share in the obligation—if I do not, at least, make an effort to practise what I have preached. In this solemn asseveration, therefore, before God and before you all, I purge my conscience of all bitterness and offence against any man, however deeply he may have injured me; and I go to that Holy Table, and I hope many of us will go to-day, in perfect charity and forgiveness, remembering what black and deep offences God, for Christ's sake, has forgiven me.'

It was the custom of the Rector on Communion morning, after the sermon was over, to move up very slowly towards the Communion Table, that he might give the principal part of the congregation who wished to leave time to do so. He did so now, but he need not have delayed; no one stirred.

The English peasant is slow, but there are moments, and those of not such infrequent occurrence as some may be disposed to think, in which he rises to an instinctive sympathy, in which I do not think that he can be beaten by any race or people upon earth.

Such a moment occurred now. 'And I hope many of us will go to-day,' — these words decided the action of the people of Clyston St. Fay. Mrs. Churchwarden Wike, acting upon some impulse which she never explained, even to her most intimate friends, put her hand upon her children to keep them in their places, and this intimation was instinctively followed throughout the whole church. No one stirred. The children — their young eyes alight with gazing upon mysteries of which they had only heard before — sat still in their places, their hands clasped before them. Many herdsmen and farm-boys, hewers of wood and drawers of water — the Gibeonites of Nature's tyranny — who never would have thought of approaching that awful table, on this day, struck and overpowered by the pervading feeling, remained at gaze.

Mr. Churchwarden Wike, very red in the face, and somewhat dim about the eyes, rose in his seat, and, in company with his fellow-warden, proceeded to collect the alms in two large silver basins, marked ·J. Y. (John Yarde), Rector, 1689.'

It was usually a very simple matter, and occupied a very short time, but to-day it taxed the efforts of the wardens considerably, and a very remarkable collection of coins, to the curious in such matters, was that presented to the Rector at the altar that day.

The Rector read the prayer for the whole state of Christ's Church Militant here on earth, the exhortation to those minded to come to the Holy Communion of the Body and Blood of our Saviour Christ, the comfortable words addressed to such, and that marvellous prayer, the suprem-est effort of divine genius, that conceives and hopes that the sinful and leprous flesh is made clean by the divine food ; and then, after the prayer of consecration and his own communicating, he made a pause.

It may strike many, doubtless, in these days, with astonishment and even disgust, but it is nevertheless a fact, that no one would have dreamt of communicating at Clyston St. Fay before the Rector's daughter had gone up.

Blanche rose in her seat. Perfectly pale, but without the slightest apparent effort or tremor, she passed up the old chancel, between the foliated scrolls of the memorials of dead rectors upon the walls, and knelt before her father in the angle of the rails. There never has been such a Communion at Clyston St. Fay either before or since.

Luncheon at the Rectory on Sundays was never a long meal, but on that day it was very short and quiet. The Rector went into his study immediately afterwards. He had hardly dared to speak to his daughter. There was something in her look that frightened him.

He had not been in his study more than a quarter of an hour, looking over his sermon for the afternoon, when a gentle tap sounded on the door, and his daughter came in. She came straight to her father, knelt down before him, and bowed her face upon his knees.

'Father,' she said, without sobbing, — 'father, I want to tell you what a wicked girl I have been. It is I who have done it all. I have ruined Mr. Damerle. He is ruined for life, and I have done it — I, and none else. I did not know — oh, I did not know it! — but I see it now. What I thought was so good in me was the worst that any girl could have been. I despised every one; I despised George Falaise. I thought no one good enough. Oh, father! I must say it — I despised you.'

He stroked her hair with his hand, so kindly and fondly that she began to sob.

'Then I saw him. I thought I loved him — I do love him now — but it was myself that I loved first. I loved him because I thought that he was like me: because he and I alone were good. I lured him on. He is ruined for life — body and soul — he is ruined for life — he who was so great and good, and it is I who have done it. Father, forgive me! God can never forgive!'

He stroked her head fondly and silently for a minute before he spoke.

'My dear, my dear,' he said, 'it is a great blow and it has unnerved you; you do not know what you say — *God* can never forgive! and yet you can say, *Father*, forgive me. You cannot tell—you are too young to know—what has occurred. You judge yourself all too harshly. You say "you lured him on." There is nothing else wanted but this to show that you are unnerved, and do not know what you say. That you despise George Falaise is a pity, for he is a fine fellow, and will prove himself such before the end. That you despised me—though not dutiful conduct for a daughter—I can better understand. May God forgive me that I have not been a better father and a better man.'

She was sobbing now passionately upon his knees.

He was frightened at her excitement and her distress.

'My dear, my dear,' he said, 'you are quite unnerved. Command yourself; I have something which I wish particularly to say.'

It would have been worth a good deal, as some men count worth, to have seen how she collected herself at these words, how she looked up into his face.

'My dear,' he said, 'I do not know what may happen to me. Life is very uncertain. You have told me that George Falaise has spoken to you. He will come back. I do not wish to

press anything upon you, but I wish to say —
life being so uncertain — that it would give me
great pleasure to see you united to George
Falaise. Now I must ask you to leave me. I
am looking over my sermon on "The Misused
Talent." I have chosen it because it is very
short.'

Blanche went down alone and sat in her seat
in the rectory pew. She never forgot that afternoon service.

The excitement of the morning had been
exhausting. and there were very few people at
church. Afterwards she used to recall it all —
the sultry summer atmosphere, the rococo classic
tablets on the walls, the sonorous rounded sentences of the sermon, Mr. Wike loyally asleep
in the churchwarden's pew. How often she
remembered it all !

She came up alone as was her wont. Mr.
Churchwarden Wike accompanied the Rector up
some minutes afterwards. He colloquied with
Mr. Binns for a minute or two in the porch.

' T' Rector seems dazed like,' he said. He
suggested that Mr. Binns might ' keep an eye
upon him.' Mr. Binns promised that he would.

When the Rector came in to dinner he seemed
to have rallied a little, and all through the meal

he evidently exerted himself to converse with his daughter. He told her one or two old-world stories of people whom he had known in his youth, which she had never heard before. He enjoined Binns to remind him of some poor people he had to visit in the morning.

He left the room as soon as dinner was over. When the gong sounded for tea he did not appear. After some little while his daughter went into the study. Her father seemed asleep in his chair; but what struck her with alarm was the sight of a book in white vellum lying, the leaves crumpled up, on the floor at his feet. She knew it to be the Aldine *Aristophanes* of 1498. However suddenly her father might have fallen asleep he would have cared for the safety of this prized book. She knelt down beside him and took his hand. He was perfectly cold. The Reverend Henry Trethellan Boteraux, Doctor of Divinity and Master of Arts, for twenty-seven years fellow and tutor of St. Nodimus College, Oxford, and Rector of Clyston St. Fay, Devonshire, was dead.

XI

THERE was a funeral at Clyston St. Fay, and another foliated monument in the chancel, and there were executors, and there was a will; all those terrible things, in short, that uproot the young life and crush the young heart.

When all this was over, it was said that there would be some two or three thousand pounds for Blanche Boteraux, and this was all. She went on a visit to her kind friends,— the clergyman's family at Bridgetown — not from her own choice, for she would have wished to have gone nowhither, but because there was nowhere else for her to go. If the cynic and the pessimist wish to find any comfort in the contemplation of human existence, which I do not suppose that they do, they might possibly find it in this thought, that in the story of the bereaved and the forsaken, in the saddest hours, such unpretentious and unfailing friends are found, of that sort with which the world is scattered over here and there, and which is the saving and the salt of it.

George Falaise was still at Oxford after the lists were out and term was ended. He shrank from leaving Oxford. It was the most perfect shelter, he felt, that he should find anywhere. He was, as he had been all his life, a lonely boy. He was premier-viscount of England, the lord of thousands of acres, which, whether they brought in any rent or not, was of no consequence to him, with coupons and consols and bank stock and every form of safe investment which the most conscientious and wealthy of trustees could contrive, but without father or mother, or brothers or sisters; practically without a home. He had no immediate relations. His father had been an only child. His mother had had one brother who died unmarried, killed in India. The nearest kin of his own age were distant cousins. He might certainly be said to be lonely, to have been lonely all his short life, and the circumstances of his life had influenced his being very much. He had few of the tastes of other men. He was the greatest *parti* of the day. If he went to a dance, the mothers and chaperons were visibly and palpably manœu-

vring, with no pretence of concealment, to secure
an introduction for their daughters and debu-
tantes — exquisite dancers many of these bewitching girls. If he accepted an invitation to
a country house, perhaps from a relation, there
were girls — girls with innocent beseeching eyes
— waylaying him in the early summer mornings
before breakfast, when he went out to smoke
a cigarette. He had not taken to drink, from
some personal idiosyncrasy he disliked the turf;
he shot, but more as a matter of duty than as
deriving much pleasure from the pursuit. If
there is nothing which you cannot have, you are
apt to care for nothing. The peculiarity of his
circumstances had made him older than his
years would imply, and had produced a lassitude
and reserve unusual in so young a man. On
one thing he had set his heart, and that thing
was denied him. Everything beside was at his
feet, even the Oxford first-class, but this one
denial poisoned all the rest. As I come to know
more of him afterwards, from living in his
house, I may be able to say more, but this much
may suffice now, to explain why he lingered at
Oxford.

He was sitting in his rooms at St. Nod's,
which he had not given up, when a late post

brought him a letter from Dr. Boteraux; one of the last letters the Rector ever wrote. The letter is before me, but I do not choose to print it. It dropped out of George Falaise's hand upon the floor.

He set his feet strongly upon the fender before him, and bore his back firmly against his chair, his hands thrust down in the pockets by his side.

'Damn him,' he said through his clenched teeth; 'I hated him from the first. My God! if I had him by the throat!'

He was of age. He had taken his degree. His guardian was too old to care, and would not interfere. There was only one thing for him to do.

But he did not count upon sudden death. The next letter he received from Devonshire was edged with deep black, and contained only a funeral card.

This second blow unnerved him altogether. He was intensely attached to the Rector, as the Rector had been to him. He had the pluck and the self-possession of his caste, but he was still only a boy. He had done a good deal; he had twice proposed to Blanche, and had been twice rejected, but he felt that he dared not see her

then. He could not have gone to the funeral,
have been in the house, without seeing her. He
did not go to the funeral; he did not even write;
he made one or two attempts and gave it up.

Bridgetown at best is not a gay place. It is
not a place to which, unless there is work given
them by the providence of God, the stricken in
Life's battle would resort for distraction or
relief.

But it would have made very little difference
to Blanche Boteraux had it been the loveliest
spot upon earth. If, instead of the dingy vicarage in the commonplace sordid street, she had
seen around her everything that art and culture
could provide. As she came down. morning
after morning, to the frugal breakfast-table, in
what might almost be called the House of
Charity, a dull sense of disappointment so complete that it crushed the soul, of a future without
hope, of the daily drag of everyday existence
that lay before her. would have taken the beauty
and the culture from any scene of earth, or
rendered them flat and unprofitable to the soul's
taste.

It may be said — I know that it has been said
— 'Why, even here, in these dull hours and lag-
ging days, there did not open to her, as to many,

stricken as she was, the glorious prospect of devoted work, — a life of nameless unrecognised self-sacrifice. of forgetfulness of the past, of singleness of purpose to press onward to the hope that is before ?'

But it did not. In place of this there was depression that can only be described as intense, sleepless nights and aimless days. As the slow hours dragged on, it seemed sometimes to Blanche Boteraux that Time itself had ceased to be, and that already the changeless monotone of a dire eternity had set in. Life and love and all fellowship and bond of life were slain in her.

There are states of being. surely, in which the past cannot be forgotten — its work cannot be undone. The issues of its unheeded hours tend to the outer darkness where there is weeping, comfortless and without end. Blanche's past, at least, could not be forgotten. for it was ever present with her. The Ideal to which she had given her whole nature could not be slain. The Idol was not shattered. Something was shattered — more things indeed than one. but the Idol remained unscathed. One of the most beautiful of English poetesses has spoken, in lines that will never die, of some whose lot is

'—to make idols and to find them clay,
And to bewail that worship ;'

but, as a matter of prosaic fact, it is very seldom,
I fancy, that a real idol is ever found to be clay.
There is something surprisingly persistent in the
existence of an idol. The one that poor Blanche
had elected to worship could not well be shattered, for it had never had any real existence in
fact. In her excited imagination it was she
who was to blame — it was she who was the
sinner.

She had been at Bridgetown for more than a
month. her state getting worse and worse. and
her friends were at a loss what to do.

'My dear,' said the good parson to his wife
one day, 'it is very difficult to know what to do.
Of course she cannot stay here for ever, and it
would not be good for her if she could. She
wants a complete change of life and scene.
What to do I do not know. She has had a
terrible shock — a series of shocks, rather —
more terrible to her than to others because of
her nature and character, and I doubt whether
her mind will ever regain its tone. She was
always of a peculiar, introspective — I should
not like to say wilful — disposition. I pity her
from my heart, but I do not know what to do.
That man, surely, will have to render a strict
account for this.'

'Well, she must stay here a little longer,' said his wife. 'Perhaps something will happen.'

She was thinking of George Falaise; but she went on —

'Perhaps some of her friends, with whom she travelled on the Continent, would take her abroad again.'

'We do not know them,' said her husband blankly; 'still, if nothing else can be done, I will write to that Miss — what was her name — who was her companion at Neufchâtel.'

But he did not write; for only two or three days after this conversation something did happen.

As I have said, Bridgetown is not a picturesque place. It stands on a dead flat, and has enjoyed just sufficient vitality and business prosperity to destroy every vestige of old-world grace and charm, and to reduce it to a dead level of commonplace ugliness. The vicarage where Blanche was staying was situated in one of the most modern, most prosaic, most squalid and unlovely parts of the town.

She was sitting alone on the morning of a dull, colourless day in a little bedroom, cheaply furnished, which she did not seem to have cared to adorn with any feminine refinements. There were a few once favourite books, but they did not seem as if they had been read for some time. Over the blind that screened the window might be seen an extensive view of slate roofs and chimney-pots and back yards, and in the extreme distance a range of low, dark woods; — a strange contrast to the scenes in which her life had hitherto been passed.

She was sitting unoccupied. looking out over the uninviting foreground, which it may be hoped that she did not see, towards these woods; but her thoughts had probably long ago passed these narrow limits. and were wandering, it surely would be unworthy to inquire where. There was a sudden knock at the door, and the house-maid, a simple Somersetshire girl, came into the room.

'Oh, miss,' she said, with an unusual defer-ence and animation, 'there is a most beautiful young gentleman in the drawing-room waiting to see you. He says his name is Lord Falaise.'

Blanche rose from her chair, and a strange kind of tremor passed over her frame as she stood looking at the girl, her hands clasped tight before her. One would have thought — and the girl did think with wonder — that something terrible, something that this strange young lady, of whom she was almost afraid, dreaded above all things, had occurred.

When she entered the drawing-room, or the simply-furnished, dull room that went by that name,—for she went downstairs after a moment's hesitation,—there certainly might seem to some persons an excuse for the girl's enthusiasm, foolish as her words might be. It was not every day in Bridgetown that you met a George Falaise. He had matured perceptibly since she had seen him last, and never can have looked better than he did at that time. He wore the light morning costume for the country of the decade,—jacket, waistcoat, leggings, and the rest, of different shaded tints, blended with quiet art. Blanche came into the room a little way, and then stopped. Neither spoke for some time.

She seemed to him, as she stood in her black dress, and her paleness and her sorrow and her distraction, more desperately beautiful than ever. His whole being went out to her with an indescribable tenderness and longing of love. He spoke first.

'I am come back,' he said; 'I shall always come back.'

She looked at him pityingly, with kindness,

like the creature of another world, as a dead
saint might be supposed to look, but she did not
speak.

'You are free,' he said. 'There is nothing
now to stand between you and me.'

Nothing! Oh, George Falaise! gallant, foolish, ignorant boy!

'Nothing!' she said; and he almost started
at her voice; it sounded so hollow and strange
to him. 'Nothing between you and me!'

She stopped and stood gazing at him, as if
wondering at such blindness; and unconsciously,
by her very action and pose, and by the look of
her eyes fixed upon him, fascinating him more
and more every second.

She herself almost forgot his presence; she
was speaking not so much to him as to some
vague questioner and phantom whom his words
had called up before her.

'Do you not know,' she went on at last, with
something almost like passion in her voice,—
'do you not know that I love him better if possible than ever? That if he sent for me now —
my God! I cannot be certain!— that I should
not go to him, wherever he might be! Cannot
you see that if I were to marry you I should
bring you nothing but sorrow, perhaps disgrace?
Nothing between you and me!'

'No,' he said, 'nothing;' and some divine feeling within him endowed him with a passion of speech beyond himself. 'You are mine now, for sorrow, and, if it must be, for disgrace. You are mine now. Nothing can separate us again. You may send me away to-day, but I shall come back. You may forbid me the house, and I shall not try to see you. I may never marry you, but I shall be near you always. You may treat me as you will, but I shall never forsake you. There must be a thousand ways, which I shall find out, by which I can support and nourish and protect you, and which you will not be able to prevent. I shall never give you up. "Je fais fort et je falaise." '

She looked at him with the kindly, the pitiful, I might almost say the loving eyes. I was wrong to say that love was slain. Love was stunned, beaten down into a state of trance or stupor, but it was not slain. She, herself, had loved so well that she knew where love was. When she saw it in his eyes, in his gesture, in the self-devotion of his speech, the sight of it was too much for her to bear. No! love was not dead, but it was not love for him.

'Oh, George, George,' she said, 'I am not worth it. I am not worthy to be so loved. I

have ruined one man, why should I ruin you?
Oh, George, let me go, let me go, let me go!'

Love aiding him with a sudden flash of something very like genius, he took these last words for a surrender.

He crossed the room to the couch on which she had sank down; he sat down and clasped her in his arms.

Stunned as she was by blow upon blow, exhausted by sleepless nights, — face to face, day and night, with a restless suffering that knew no respite, with an aching sense of misery that never for a moment ceased, — she sank upon his breast.

PART II

I

When I first knew Lord and Lady Falaise, they had been married about twelve years. There was a very quiet wedding at Bridgetown; the bride was married in her travelling dress. What sort of thrill convulsed London society when the news became public I do not know, but Lord Falaise never forgot the friends from whose house he had married his wife. He took his bride to Hawkridge St. Mary, the Duke's house, where they stayed for a fortnight. The Duke, who was very old and feeble, was exceedingly taken with Blanche. 'Falaise,' he said from his armchair, as they were about leaving the drawing-room on the first night of their arrival, his valet standing by his side to take him away as soon as they had left the room, — 'Falaise, you have got a wife of whom any man might be proud;' and indeed she looked very well in her low dress of dull black silk.

There was something about the old man, his courtesy and his old-world talk, that touched her very closely, that reminded her of her father, and associated itself with a thought that made life bitter, with her passionate regret that she had not valued that father as she might have done.

Hawkridge St. Mary was a beautiful little estate which the Duke had purchased for himself, the ducal mansions being Palladian in their architecture, and very painful in their domestic arrangements. It has woods and a deer-park and an old timbered mansion, with cosy panelled rooms, and oak staircases and galleries. Some months afterwards, when the Duke died, it was found that he had left this property to Blanche.

'It's Falaise's wife, I mean,' he said to his solicitor from his couch; and whether he knew at the moment which Falaise it was — his godson or his old friend — the lawyer did not think it necessary to inquire.

They did not keep the place. The new Duke was bitterly disappointed at losing this gem of a house, and it seemed hardly fair to let the passing fancy of a very old man, however kindly, deprive his successor of it. An arrangement was made by which it was exchanged for a villa on the Riviera — a property of inferior value, but which might prove to be useful, though in fact it never did.

But a still more astonishing event occurred about a year after the marriage, for the final judgment in the protracted suit was given in favour of the heirs of the Rev. Dr. Boteraux. There were considerable estates, but the personality was sworn under one hundred and fifty thousand pounds.

After the visit to Hawkridge the Falaises went abroad, where they remained for more than two years, and where both their boys were born. I have talked. at Trefennick, with an old servant — maid, nurse, and housekeeper — and she has told me that her lady was always much better abroad. 'When the boys were very little, mere babies,' she said, 'Lady Falaise seemed to take great pleasure and delight in them, as another woman would; but as they grew bigger, and when the family returned to England, she seemed to lose this interest. "They were Lord Falaise's boys," she used to say. It was always "Lord Falaise." "Lord Falaise likes this, or wishes that."' This woman has told me that she has known her lady to watch her husband during the whole day, to find out what he really wished about any particular scheme or plan. This was precisely how she struck me when I first knew her.

'The boys are Lord Falaise's boys,' she said, very early in our acquaintance. 'They resemble him in everything—disposition, feature, character. They will grow up to be great and noble, as he is.'

I had not come to the house many times, reading French with the boys, and teaching them the violin, for which neither possessed any remarkable talent, when Lady Falaise showed an unmistakable liking for me, and for having me with her. The servants said that they had never seen her so well or so interested before. Since the children were babies she had never shown so much interest in them as she did now, in their French, and in their very crude attempts on the violin.

If I am asked to account for this singular partiality for a stranger. I can only say that I think it was principally owing to my foreign extraction and training. Blanche Falaise had been much attracted to foreign society of a certain kind, and to foreign thought, in her girlhood, and I think that something about me recalled to her the freshness and interest of those early bright days, before the fatal blow had fallen which had marred her life.

One day Lord Falaise spoke to me. He said that he could not be grateful enough for the pleasure I had brought into his wife's life, and for the comparative interest in outward affairs which my coming had seemed to excite in her. He begged that I would come and stay in the house permanently. 'You would come.' he said. 'in every respect on the standing of a most valued guest.' It goes without saying that I agreed to this proposal. and from that day to the death of Lady Falaise. I scarcely slept a night apart from the family.

It will be easily understood that I took a lively interest in my kind patrons, and in all that concerned them. We lived principally at Trefennick. It was a matter of perfect indifference to herself where Lady Falaise lived in England. Society was a burden to her, though she rose to the necessities of such entertainment with an unsurpassable grace. Lord Falaise was very fond of the estate. He was a popular but autocratic landlord. He spent exceptional sums on repairs. and on labourers' cottages with allotment gardens. on drainage and improvements; and he was most forbearing to a favourite tenant, forgiving almost anything to keep him, as he would say, on the land; but he must be a tenant after his own mind. He would never cut down a tree, nor demolish an old building if he could help it. He would interest himself exceedingly in procuring old tiles for the repair of the roofs of ancient mills and cattle-sheds. He resisted a local authority, of some kind, for years, over an improvement on the King's highway, because the proposed alteration would spoil a picturesque turn of the road, and he was in constant hot water with other authorities, over cutting the overhanging boughs of trees in his lanes. He did not seem to care for many things that I should have expected him to care for. Racing he took no pleasure in. I always thought that he shot more as a matter of duty than of pleasure; I have been told that he was a very good shot. He did not care for the Riviera. 'Too many people there,' he said; 'princes and millionaires and people of that sort.' I have heard him called a prig. It pained me very much at first, until I remembered that I have heard Sir Charles Grandison called a prig, and by very nice people too.

Sometime in the summer, after I became a member of the family, the house was very full of company. There was among the party a doctor, a married man of between thirty and forty, who took a great fancy to me. I believe he complimented me with believing that I was able to appreciate his talk. He was a great talker. I have always divided men into two classes: those who talk in the evening — and these are by far the most numerous — and those brilliant few whom I have always admired, who talk at breakfast. Dr.——(I have forgotten his name) talked incessantly. He always contrived to sit by me at breakfast; but, not content with this, he would insist on my taking a turn with him in the long yew walk after breakfast, talking the whole time.

'What a perfectly delightful creature Lady Falaise is!' he said; 'I suppose you have been her friend from childhood. She is evidently *raffoler* on you.'

I endeavoured to interpose some explanation, but without success. 'Ah yes, yes!' he went on; 'you know her story, of course. I should be very anxious about her if I were her husband. Through all that winsome grace of manner, that devotion to the meanest guest, I can recognise a disordered mind; I can detect a lurking despair. The strain cannot endure for ever, the cord must snap sometime, and then? Lord Falaise now, what an absolute contrast! I do not know how it has struck you, Miss Wand (he certainly never gave himself any time to learn), but I always regard him as the perfect example of a noble, the most complete egoist it is possible to conceive.'

'Egoist!' I said, indignantly.

'Ah yes, yes!' he said, waving me off; 'I understand your objection, but I use the word in its strictly scientific sense. I look upon the true egoist as the perfect man. The most perfect egoist is God.'

'That seems to me a strange, not to say a doubtful expression,' I managed to interpolate.

'Ah! that is because you scarcely realise what an egoist really is — a man absorbed in the one conception, as to what it becomes him — himself — to do and to be. I feel morally certain that in Lord Falaise's secret heart he is profoundly convinced that the whole tendency of intelligent being, the entire effort of creative action from, at least, the commencement of the palæozoic period, has concentrated itself as its supreme result somewhere about George 27th Viscount Falaise.'

He paused a moment for breath, and I own I

could not suppress a faint smile. Thus encouraged he went on —

'But where is the harm — nay, rather, is there not an infinite good? This superb egoism, so far from being prejudicial to himself or to others, is for both an unspeakable gain, a priceless possession. To himself it gives what to other men would seem an unattainable ideal — nothing can be unattainable to George 27th Viscount Falaise. As to others, you are perhaps best able to judge how this nature, sweetened by prosperity, cultivated and taught to act by this egoistic ideal, benefits those around him.'

'I should hesitate to say "sweetened by prosperity,"' I broke in; 'the one desire of his heart is denied him.'

'That is true,' he said, — 'that is quite true; but I alluded to mundane prosperity, which is a wonderful lenitive to some natures. Some people may be deceived by his simple, unaffected, modest manner — I do not mean you or I, Miss Wand,' he said with a smile; 'but if any coarser nature doubts what I say, I should recommend him, by way of testing the truth of it, *to take a liberty* with Lord Falaise. Only I should wish to be warned beforehand. I do not like the disagreeable, and absent myself from it where and when I can.'

When there was no company in the house, we — Lady Falaise and I — used to sit mostly in her boudoir — a lovely room which she had made her own, or rather which Lord Falaise had arranged for her in an angle of the south front. It commanded views in two directions — into the wooded dingles of the park, and over the distant reaches of the plain.

It may be supposed that we avoided all mention of Mr. Damerle, but the exact opposite of this was the fact. On one of the first occasions on which we sat together, in this room, Lady Falaise began upon the subject herself —

'You have heard all about my miserable story, Miss Wand,' she said; she had wanted me to call her "Blanche," and she would call me Claire, and because I declined, she insisted for some time on calling me Miss Wand, — 'of course you have heard all about it. I want you to understand that it was all my fault. I wish you to understand that it was I who was utterly and entirely to blame. I was eaten up with spiritual pride. I thought myself very good, and, still more, very clever too. No one was good or clever enough for me. When I saw Mr. Damerle first, I endowed him with all the virtues and gifts which I believed that I myself possessed. I was pleased and flattered by his attention. I thought that he alone was worthy of me, and that he recognised at a glance that I alone was worthy of him. My pleasure, and my admiration of him, lured him on. It was my fault.'

I could not help looking at her with a kind of anger, yet with wondering pity. It seemed a strange perversion of fact and of blame.

'It is difficult for me to look at it in that light,' I said ; 'at any rate, whatever fault there may have been on your side, the proportion of suffering has been very unjustly meted out. Mr. Damerle appears to have suffered nothing. He has married a rich and titled lady. He has been living, all these years, a life of public praise and honour, and he is supposed to be working most successfully in the Highest Cause a man can work in. He appears to me to have suffered nothing, and to endure no punishment at all.'

I spoke bitterly, as, I hope, it is natural that one woman should speak of a wrong done to another.

The expression of Lady Falaise's face seemed to me very beautiful as she spoke again — so beautiful, indeed, that I looked at her with surprise.

'If I thought that,' she said; 'it would make all the difference in my life. If I thought that his conscience was at peace, and that he was happy, I might be a happy mother and wife; but I do not believe it—for a single second I could not believe it. No, not even in a dream.'

I did not say anything, but waited for her to go on. But she did not say anything for some time. She sat looking straight before her, as though some distinct vision had passed before her eyes, then she said—

'No; it cannot be that. He was too great, too noble, for that. There are some deeds that such a man as he is can never overlive. He is ruined, body and soul; and it is through me.'

I began to understand what she meant.

'I see,' I said; 'the captive exile hasteneth that he should not die in the pit.'

'But how can he escape?' she said passionately; 'how can he breathe freely even, while I am alive?'

'Your death would make no difference,' I said; 'the deed would have been done all the same.'

'Do you ever hear of him?' I said, after a pause, as she did not speak again.

'No,' she said; 'I never go to London, and

I never see the papers — not even the Church papers; Lord Falaise never mentions his name. I pray day and night.' she went on with a passionate eagerness. 'that Lord Falaise may not hate him; but I fear that he does.'

There was another pause, after which she said —

'He married a Lady Elizabeth Poer, the daughter of a Scottish earl; she was said to have a large fortune; but these things are often exaggerated, and a great deal of money does not go far in London.'

It was only a few days after this talk that I went one morning, after my lesson on the violin, into the morning room or 'saloon,' as it was called at Trefennick, to look at the local daily papers. The London papers did not reach Trefennick till the next morning by post; but the *Western Morning News* and some other local papers arrived during the morning, brought by a boy and his pony from the nearest station, and they always lay in the morning room. Opening one of these papers, the first paragraph that caught my eye was the announcement that the Rev. Paul Damerle, Rector of some church in London near the Regent's Park, would preach on a week-day afternoon at the Cathedral at

Minsterley on the occasion of the annual festival of some hospital.

I looked no further into the paper. My thoughts were all absorbed by this single paragraph. What should I do? Should I let things take their course? Should I wait till Lord Falaise, in the natural course of things, saw the paragraph, and let him tell his wife or not as he chose? But Lady Falaise had been so good to me, she had so trusted me, she had confided her inmost mind so fully to me, that it seemed disloyal and base to keep anything that touched her so nearly — anything that I had chanced to become acquainted with — from her for a moment. I took the paper in my hand and went upstairs.

'Lady Falaise,' I said, 'there is something here that will interest you. I have only just opened the paper.'

She was sitting in that lovely room, which her husband had arranged for her, with a pale yellow embossed paper that threw up the ebony and ivory cabinets; above which, on the upper part of the walls, festoons of Indian silk lined the room, and framed windows which were in themselves pictures of exquisite beauty.

Distinct lines and shades of woodland, losing

themselves in dark masses of more distant wood, and beyond this, in faultless gradation, tints, changed and softened into delicate blues, and, still refining and more refined, into a line of stainless white that marked the infinite horizon, and then returning in answering gradations of delicate blues, becoming more and more intense overhead, till in the sky above, instead of the waving greenwood, the pure deep summer azure defied the puny sight to fathom its depths. All this I saw mechanically during the moment that Lady Falaise glanced at the paper and gave it back to me.

'Claire,' she said, 'I should like to hear him again,—I fear that it will annoy Lord Falaise that he should be so near—but I should like to hear him again. I never knew him but when he was good. To me, whenever I saw him, until that terrible letter which was not himself, he was nothing but what was noble and good. I should like to hear him again.'

'It will bring up the old miserable story again,' I said, 'if you are seen there.'

'I should like to hear him again,' she said; 'I will speak to Lord Falaise.'

What persuasive argument she used I do not know. It was so seldom that she wished for anything — so seldom that anything that could be thought of as self-pleasing could be associated with her — that I fancy that her husband's delight at finding anything that she really wished for overbore every other thought. It was nothing to him what other people would say or think. In a day or two Lady Falaise told me that we were to go to Minsterley, to a cousin of her husband's, a Lady Hele, an elderly lady who lived in Minsterley, in the Close. I was to accompany them of course, she said; Lady Hele particularly wished to see Blanche's friend.

We travelled to Minsterley on the morning of the day on which the sermon was to be preached at the Minster, and arrived at Lady Hele's in time for luncheon. She lived in a beautiful old house, which possessed a delightful drawing-room, one window of which looked upon the trees in the Bishop's garden, and the other upon the great east window and the Minster towers. Lady Hele struck me at once as possessing a peculiarity I have constantly noticed in women of rank belonging to the Devon and Cornish families, — a peculiarity which I attribute, in great measure, to their climate — a peculiar soft-ness and sweetness, combined with a freshness and piquancy, singularly reminding one of the breezes of their own moors and combes.

'I hope you will not mind,' I heard her say to Lord Falaise; 'but I have asked a few people to dinner. We so seldom see you and Blanche that I could not resist such a temptation.'

By three o'clock we were assembled in the Minster, the nave of which was crowded from end to end. There was a shortened evening service, and then the preacher entered the pulpit. I was very well placed for seeing him. and was, I confess, very much struck by his appearance, which was more attractive than I had expected. His expression was more refined and less harsh and set than I had anticipated.

I have already attempted to describe more than one of Mr. Damerle's sermons. which I did not myself hear, but I shall not attempt to describe this one. I will only say that it thrilled and impressed the crowded audience through and through. I doubt if there was a single person in the Minster who was altogether untouched by it. It was not only that the fervour and eloquence were remarkable; there ran through these impassioned sentences a strange graphic reality that was startling and even painful. One felt from moment to moment as though the preacher was about to reveal some shameful confession, either on his own behalf or on that of others. A strained expectation, almost dread, followed him through these rapid and fervid passages, as one follows, or rather is swept along in the rush and tumult of some great sonata. He wound up with a withering denunciation of the conventional charities and the paltry self-denials of ordinary life.

We were coming out of the Minster in the dense throng. Blanche Falaise was a little in advance with Lady Hele, and was separated from us by the crowd. I was close to Lord Falaise when I was aware of a tall, distinguished-looking young man, with clear, well-cut features, but a hard unpleasant expression of face, who was pressed close to us by the throng.

'Ah, Falaise!' he said, with an indolent, supercilious drawl, 'you go with the multitude! Not much in our line, is it?'

'Speak for yourself,' said Lord Falaise. 'I thought it was very striking.'

'Oh, striking enough!' said the other. 'I wonder,' he went on, after a moment's pause, and perceptibly sinking his voice,—'I wonder how much of that spiritual fervour, that thrilling tone, that descriptive power, is due to port wine?'

Lord Falaise looked at him with a sudden interest.

'Oh! that's it, is it?' he said.

'Oh! and worse,' said the other. 'Debts and the devil to pay; I should not be surprised to hear of anything. Sorry for Lady Elizabeth — knew her when I was a boy.'

The crowd seemed to fade from my eyes as I looked eagerly before me to see if it were possible for Lady Falaise to have heard, but she was almost hidden from sight some feet in advance of us, and I do the young man simple justice when I say that he spoke very low.

'Well, ta-ta,' he said. 'Thanks, no. Won't speak to Lady Falaise to-day. She would not be in the humour to listen to me,' and he edged his way apart from us through the crowd.

'Can it possibly be true?' I said.

'I should not wonder. That is Lord Cheddersley, the Earl of Cheddersley — racing, gambling, money-lenders at his finger ends. He would be a likely man to know.'

Oh! dear, dear Lady Falaise!

WHEN we joined Lady Hele and Blanche outside the western door, we certainly found that Lady Falaise was not in the humour to have listened to Lord Cheddersley's society talk. I had never before seen her look so radiant and full of life. It revealed to me something of how she must have looked in the old days. There was not much said. Some of us had something else now to think of, and for the rest, it seemed as if the sermon had so impressed itself upon all hearts that we could speak of nothing else, and not much even of that. We returned to Lady Hele's. where we found afternoon tea, and two or three other ladies followed us in.

One of these, evidently a gossipy sort of person, began speaking immediately to Lady Hele.

'They are staying with Lady Doone,' she said. 'It was she really who brought him down. I'm told there was great opposition to it on the committee — all the county members opposed it, but the townspeople carried it. Lady Doone must have a lion every now and then, don't you know.'

The words were scarcely out of her mouth when the door of the long drawing-room was thrown open, and the butler announced —

'Lady Doone, Mr. and Lady Elizabeth Damerle.'

Lady Doone came forward eagerly. She was a small gushing person, not, I believe, a Devonshire woman by birth.

'Dear Lady Hele!' she said, 'I thought I must bring them to see you!'

Then her eyes fell on Lord Falaise, and, glancing round the room she saw Blanche also, and she began evidently to perceive that she had made a mistake.

There was a somewhat awkward silence in the room. Then Lord Falaise came up and shook hands with her cordially. and Mr. Damerle, who was close behind in advance of his wife. looked very much as if he were going to offer him his hand. He, however, thought better of it, and contented himself with saying —

'I have met Lord Falaise before.'

'Yes,' said Lord Falaise; 'I have met Mr. Damerle before.'

There are different ways of saying a few simple words. There was nothing further needed after Lord Falaise had said these.

'Lady Elizabeth,' said Lady Doone, recovering herself.

She came forward and shook hands with the lady of the house,—a tall woman, with the remains of beauty, but aged evidently before her time, and with a wan, hunted look in the pale eyes that struck me to the heart, for I remembered something like it in my mother's face.

I did not like Mr. Damerle's look so well as I had done in the Minster. He coarsened perceptibly upon a nearer view, and there was a wavering uncertain look about him, as though he were not altogether sure of his ground.

Then a thing happened, so strange, that I believe no one present would have believed it if they had not seen it with their eyes. Blanche Falaise came across the room with her hand stretched out and a look of radiant welcome in her face.

'Mr. Damerle and I,' she said, 'are very old friends.'

My God! I thought, has she forgotten what

she has said to me — that he is ruined, body and soul?

He kept his self-possession marvellously well, and said something to her in a low voice.

As I stood watching them, I remembered that she had also said that, could she suppose that he was happy and good, she might even still become a happy mother and a happy wife. Had the sermon worked this hallucination upon her? Did she really dream that so it was? Oh poor, poor Lady Falaise!

After Lady Doone and her guests had left, for they did not stay long. pleading other visits before dinner, and we were leaving the drawing-room, Lord Falaise was close to me —

'Did you notice that woman's eyes?' he said; 'can you doubt Cheddersley's story now?'

Lady Hele's 'few people' turned out to be a large dinner-party of some twenty people. The hostess went in with the Dean, next to him sat Blanche Falaise, and by her, and nearly opposite to me, sat a most beautiful old man — General Sir Gifford Limoge, who had won his majority in the old Sikh war. One sleeve hung useless by his side, but he fed himself with marvellous

deftness with one hand; and through his kindly
courteous manner, as he spoke to Blanche, and
through the soft, fatherly glance of the gray,
pleasant eyes, there might still be seen, by those
who knew how to look for them, some glimpses
of the fire and strength that had carried him
through that war of the Titans, when the fate
of a universe hung in the balance, and the line
was broken at Chillianwallah.

Towards the end of dinner, my immediate
neighbour being occupied with Lady Hele, I was
occupied in watching this beautiful old man,
who was now talking to the lady on his right,
with ever increasing admiration, when I was
suddenly attracted by a voice which I had heard
as a jarring note more than once during the
meal.   It proceeded from a gentleman seated a
little farther down the table on the opposite
side to that on which I sat, and therefore on the
same side with Blanche — a cabinet minister of
the new school.

I had noticed this voice at intervals during
dinner, — a hard, rasping voice that dominated
every other sound in its immediate neighbourhood. There was something about the man
different from any other at the table, — a something apart from a nameless fellowship that

marked the rest — a sort of palpable ignorance and ineptitude as to the otherwise understood *convenance* of place and time.

'I am told,' he was saying, 'that it is quite a scandal that he was allowed to preach at all. It is gone so far as that. I am told that he has wasted all his wife's fortune, that he ill-treats her, that he drinks — in fact, that his voice, his manner, his eloquence, are simply the result of port wine.'

Sitting exactly opposite this man was a very intimate friend of Lord Falaise, whom I just knew by sight, a Mr. Senlac, a permanent official in some Government office, a man of peculiar distinction of appearance, both in expression and contour. He made a gallant but desperate attempt to retrieve this fatal blunder.

'Ah, you are alluding to that person in London! I saw it in the paper the other day;' and I felt, rather than saw, from the side glance which alone I had of the striking face, that he gave this blundering statesman a look which, one might have thought, would have enlightened any man, but it did not enlighten this one.

'No, I'm not,' replied the strident voice; 'I am speaking of the man who preached in the

Cathedral this afternoon, before the *élite* of Devonshire — the Rev. Paul Damerle.'

Lady Hele stood up, and we all rose. I looked across at Blanche with a terrible dread of what might happen. She rose mechanically and stood for a second or two perfectly rigid and white, the tips of her fingers resting on the table before her. All the blood in her veins seemed to have left the body and to have retreated elsewhere, leaving her cold and dead. Her eyes were fixed. The thought struck me, at the moment, that she was like a person shot through the heart, whose body stands for a moment, dead, before it falls. But she did not fall; after a second or two she seemed to recover consciousness, to control herself. She passed round the end of the table, the tips of the fingers of one hand still resting upon it, to Lady Hele, who took her arm. I stepped back a little way to let them pass, and followed them and the other ladies out of the room.

When we reached the drawing-room she sat down in the shade, a little behind Lady Hele, and remained quite silent. The conversation flagged a little at first. It required some little time to dismiss the overpowering thought that occupied all minds; but the feat was accomplished in a few minutes, assisted considerably by the advent of coffee. The gentlemen were not long in coming up. I fancied that they had found it more difficult than we had to relapse into ordinary talk. Lord Falaise looked pale, and glanced anxiously round as he came in. Some days afterwards I asked him what they had done.

'Oh! I went up to the other end of the table and talked to the Dean and Sir Gifford,' he said; 'Senlac behaved beautifully, of course. He talked "procedure" across the table to Mr. —— in a loud voice. What would have happened without him I don't know. No one else, I think, felt equal to speaking to him. I doubt whether he has the least idea what he did even now.'

So, as all evenings do, even that evening came to an end at last.

WE went back to Trefennick the next day. There was no reason why we should not do so; but apart from other and obvious reasons, I think that Lord Falaise was rather anxious about his boys. I fancy that his peculiar theory about home education was breaking down. The boys were only eleven and twelve. Their father taught them Latin and the Greek verbs, and he rode out with them every day. It was a very pretty sight to see them together — the beautiful ponies the boys had, and Lord Falaise's cob. I used to go to the great hall door to see them start, but I could very seldom persuade Blanche to come.

I cannot tell how it was. At this distance of time, even, I do not know. It seemed that she could fulfil her duty at other times, that she could bear anything rather than this.

But, at any rate, Lord Falaise arrived at the

conclusion that his boys would be better at Eton than at home, in the country, alone. They should both, being so near of an age, go to Eton together. The second boy was rather more forward than the elder. It was decided that they should go to school after Christmas.

Up and down the great yew walk, in the mild September days, I paced with Blanche, when she poured out to me her whole heart — the depth of self-condemnation, the longing, the passionate yearning to save this man. I bore it for a long time, but at last I could restrain myself no longer, and I spoke out —

'You are committing,' I said, 'a terrible, almost a nameless sin. You are trying to take this man's sin, this man's punishment, upon yourself. There is only One who can do that.'

I do not think that my words had any effect upon her at all. There are some natures, especially among women, who, like the old-time yew trees beside which we walked, seem to belong to themselves alone, — that is to say, that, for evil or for good, they press on for the mark that is set before them, turning neither to the right hand nor to the left. Through the valley of the shadow of death — strange cries and voices in their ears — they press on, impassive and unmoved. I think that Blanche Falaise was such as these. The yew hedges, century after century, remain at their post, the guardian and the shelter of slight beings almost as ephemeral as the gnats that dance around their boughs; just so the slight, delicate woman, in the midst of life's turmoil, is not alone. Certainties and Realities and Powers — a science of being unerring and eternal as Fate — environ her, and guard her, and urge her on.

One morning, when two or three gentlemen were staying at Trefennick for the shooting, as we were leaving the breakfast-table, Lord Falaise said to me —

'Lord Cheddersley is shooting to-day with a German prince. They are to lunch with us some miles from here, and Blanche is so good as to join us. I hope that you will come.'

Outside the room, in the great hall, was the principal coachman in undress, a man of whom I stood in the greatest awe.

'Oh, Fisher,' said Lord Falaise, — 'yes, yes, Lord Cheddersley is shooting over the Dornton farms with the Prince von Leuthen-Stalrenberg. They will lunch with us at the bailiff's house at

Braynes. You will drive her ladyship and Miss Wand there. You know the lanes. We shall be there at two o'clock.'

'Yes, my lord.'

As we were going up the staircase, Blanche said to me —

'You had better put on your best things. Lord Falaise will like it.'

I made myself look as nice as I could, my French mother's instinct helping me ; but I confess that I was astonished when Lady Falaise came down the great staircase into the hall to get into the carriage, to see how wonderfully beautiful she was. She was dressed in a close-fitting cloth of peacock blue, edged with small peacock feathers, and a hat to match ; with the lovely colouring of her fair brown hair, and the sad, far-off look in her gray-brown eyes, she seemed to me at that moment the most lovely creature that the world had ever seen. It was one of those days in autumn which summer, like a regal donor, flings back out of his abundance to console the lingering, gaping crowd left at gaze by his dazzling train. We drove out in the soft, warm, midday air, down the slopes of the drive, shadowed by the great oaks, out through the old iron gates of the park, with the quick-stepping, smooth motion of the beautiful horses, through lanes of high-banked, faded fern and bryony, and pale, late-born flowers, surprised and benighted in the autumn hours upon which their birth had been cast, over the first fallen and withered leaves, and through running streams of clear, brown water, seeking their way from the boggy moorlands to the plain. An indescribable sense of rest and peace hung over the faded landscape, in the soft blue of the cloud-flecked sky, in the hush of the wide pastures; over the spreading woods of fading chestnuts and sycamores, and the bright, dying colouring of the ashes, and the still, warm summer tints of the oaks and elms; over the churches and old halls, and houses standing in courtyards, with lichen and faded stonecrop and wallflowers upon the tiled roofs and upon the walls; over the homesteads and groups of cottages in flowery gardens, whence the children ran to see the carriage pass.

At last we came out into a more champaign country, where the sense of seclusion and stillness and peace gave place to a wider instinct and a larger vision and desire. Before us, beyond the sunny slopes, there lay a region of brilliant light and deep shadow, of which the dazzled sense knew not whether it were earth or heaven, or woodland or sky; and amid the waving lines of this mystic sea, which, by some instinct, one felt was teeming with a hidden life of human effort and promise, we could see the flash of sunshine upon the church towers, the faint mist over village and town, the deeper flush of stately parks, the dark line of moorland hiding mysteries of wild solitudes, and bleak prisons, and haunts of reckless despair.

Through all this wonderful beauty — this peace and calm, this widespread life and hope — Blanche Falaise lay back in the great carriage perfectly impassive, silent, and unmoved.

On the nearer slopes before us, between the openings of the hedgerows and the woods, there had appeared, from time to time, curls of white smoke, and I noticed that Fisher timed himself very accurately as to his pace, sometimes slackening almost to a walk, sometimes increasing his speed. He attained, in fact, to such a pitch of accuracy that, as we turned the corner of a wooded lane and came out upon a broader path, with grass on either side, where two lanes crossed, and saw before us, at the junction of the roads, a picturesque house, apparently of considerable antiquity, the converging parties of sportsmen, who had evidently timed themselves also, appeared upon the green. They came up the cross road in opposite directions, and the chief gentlemen on either side raised their low-crowned hats as they approached each other. The next moment we drove up.

There was considerable excitement; I was presented to His Royal Highness. Lady Falaise had met him before. He was a pleasant, fair young man, with a gracious, winning manner.

'I speak English tolerably,' he said to me at lunch; 'but I do not understand it quite so well.'

I told him I thought that there were many, home-born, who would sympathise with him in that respect.

We went into the picturesque old house, through a quaint, panelled passage, into a kind of large kitchen or hall. Across the ceiling were vestiges of plaster-work, together with white-washed beams, which seemed to indicate a past history. A wide, open hearth occupied nearly one side of the room, upon which was a large iron pot simmering over a fire of wood. Small leaden panes let in a dim light through one or two long low windows at the end of the room; a large oaken chest or coffer, with some seventeenth century date, such as one sees in cottages, was covered with delicate napery, and piled with cold meats and ancient silver flagons containing ale; and in this old-world farmroom we sat down to the most exquisite and luxurious lunch I had ever seen. Nearly all the servants at Trefennick were there. A succession of the most delicate entrées and costliest wines seemed to blend or to contrast with the rough rustic surrounding, as in the tissue of some piece of tapestry the fine gossamer threads, with their weft of dainty colour, merge and melt into the background of the broader and more fearless textures of warp and woof.

I sat by the prince, who, of course, was mostly occupied with Lady Falaise. Lord Cheddersley sat on Blanche's other hand, Lord Falaise at the other end of the table among the men. A young man, who sat at my other side, began to talk at once.

'I thought we arranged our meeting very well, didn't you? I hope Falaise was pleased. Cheddersley was awfully nervous: never thought he could be nervous. "We must break off, gentlemen," he said; "we have just time. Falaise is such a very particular man. If we are a minute late, I shouldn't wonder if he gave up shooting for the rest of the day, and that would be a pity. I'm told that his farms are alive with partridges. Falaise shoots very little; he is too great a man to do anything very much." So we had to come. I hope Falaise was pleased.'

I looked at my companion more closely, and thought that I had seen him before. He was a slight, delicate-looking young man, with a pleasant, almost childlike expression of face, but with a sharply-defined outline, a well-cut, prominent nose, and an infinitely dainty little moustache. He had a way of raising his eyebrows which gave him a look of almost babyish innocence. He wore a shooting costume of fine shades of leather and corduroy, of a careful, almost finikin style.

'Have you not been at Trefennick?' I said; 'I think I have seen you there.'

'Oh yes!' he said very modestly; 'I remember you very well. I have a little Property in this neighbourhood — three or four farms — and I come down twice a year to collect my Rents.'

He had a trick of dwelling on the initial consonant of all important words, which was very effective.

'I am staying at Cheddersley's,' he went on. 'Cheddersley is very kind. Most astonishing how kind People are. Never could understand why people pay you any rent. Why should they? Don't tell them please, but my tenants always astonish me. I assume a *dégagé* manner, don't you know, as though it were the most natural thing in the world; but it always astonishes me.'

'I have no doubt that you are a very good landlord,' I said politely.

'Oh, they say that I am a gentleman!' he said, smiling. 'I am very proud of that. They always say that. "Whatever comes of it," they say, "they will say that;" and I always take off everything they ask. I am so astonished at their paying anything. Suppose they didn't? What could I do?'

'Would it not be better if you employed an agent?' I said.

'No,' he said slowly. 'I beg your pardon, Miss Wand, but I think not. I have known men who did that. They had all their farms thrown on their hands. They had to take to farming. They didn't make much of that. They had no tenants to pay them any rents. And, really, Miss Wand, my people take off very little

— very little indeed. I assure you I go back loaded with untold gold — gold and notes and cheques. And they give me beer, too, always; never drink such beer as they give me. Won't you try some of this anchovy toast ? — it is Perfectly crisp — and bread and cheese ; never get such bread in London, and all for nothing ! It is a very Puzzling world, Miss Wand,' he said very solemnly, looking down upon his plate — ' you may take my word for it — a very Puzzling world.'

The day was very warm for the season, and we were glad to come out upon the green as soon as possible after lunch.

We stood about upon the mossy turf amid the stillness and peace of the early afternoon, amid the falling leaves, the groups of gentlemen standing about smoking, the dogs lying down or wandering restlessly to and fro. The prince was standing by me talking pleasantly in German, which he had found out that I knew. Lord and Lady Falaise and Lord Cheddersley had wandered out, as it seemed by some concerted plan, down the wide lane for some five minutes or so, until the carriage drove up. As they came back towards us, I could see that Blanche was greatly moved. Lord Cheddersley seemed to be speaking eagerly, and, as it seemed to me, with a more sincere endeavour to do right than I should have been inclined to give him credit for. She came up to us walking between the two — Lord Falaise very sad and still — her hands clasped before her. The appalling beauty of her steadfast face, set in the delicate shading and the matchless colouring of her dress, and the background of green sward and faded hedgerow, reminded me again of some old-world tapestry work, making a picture of Our Lady of grief.

As she came near the carriage, which by this time had driven up, she seemed by a supreme effort to recall herself to the duties of the moment. She spoke to the prince in German, with a sweetness which evidently fascinated him; she said something equally gracious to several other gentlemen who stood by, and then we got into the carriage and waited while the gentlemen regained their guns, and, this time in a collected group, passed over into the fields, more in the direction from which we had come in the morning. Then we drove off slowly, Fisher pulling up now and then at some lane-side gate, whence we might see the line of white puffs of smoke, along the sloping fields, or the ridges of wood and copse.

Blanche Falaise lay back in the carriage; she evidently saw nothing of the shooting or of the sloping fields; she put her left hand upon my lap, as if feeling, as it were, for a friendly grasp. There was something unspeakably touching in the action and in the craving need that prompted the gesture.

'Oh, he has told us the most terrible things! Lord Cheddersley says that he will be imprisoned on a charge of fraud. Sin is at the bottom of it, and the sin is mine.'

I grasped her hand tightly in mine.

'I will not hear what you say,' I said passionately. 'I will not listen to you for a moment longer. You are trying, as I told you before, to take this man's sin and punishment upon yourself. You cannot do it. The thought of such a thing even is a terrible, a nameless sin.'

'No,' she said. 'I am not mistaken. Would to God I were! Others may sin and suffer for it; but they could not have sinned if I had not sinned first. My sin, which no one blames—of which perhaps no one knows—no one! O my God!'

She was deathly pale, as she had been that night of the dinner—all the blood seemed to have left her body. She sat in the carriage like a corpse.

All around us, beneath the autumnal sky, more entrancing in its wan beauty than the loveliest colouring of summer, lay the autumn landscape, with here and there the late sheaves and the pale woodlands, with their recollection of a beauty more lovely than beauty ever was. '*Veteris vestigia flammæ*' I once saw written somewhere. I hardly know, but I fancy that it means something low and poor compared to these autumn woods; but it always seemed to me that the rhythm of the Latin sound, more than any poem, suited such a scene; and in the midst of all this beauty she sat, silent and inert, — she, Lady Falaise, a more miserable woman than could have been found that day in the most terrible — for I know them — of the London slums.

IV

IT was about a fortnight after this luncheon
that Lady Falaise opened a letter one morning
at breakfast, which she immediately handed to
her husband, and which he, in response to a
gesture from her, passed on to me.

Lady Elizabeth Damerle wishes to see Lady Falaise
for a few moments. She does not wish for any entertainment, only for a quarter of an hour's interview.
Unless she hears to the contrary, she will come on Tues-
day the 17th; and if Lady Falaise would be so kind as
to send a carriage to Branscombe Station to meet the
train that stops there at 3.5 P.M., it would be a great
kindness. Lady Elizabeth Damerle would not make this
request, but she does not know any other means of reaching Trefennick.

27 Chertsey Gardens, W.S.

To this somewhat strange letter an immediate
answer was sent —

Lady Falaise will be delighted to see Lady Elizabeth
Damerle at the time she names. A carriage shall be sent
to meet the train at Branscombe at 3.5 P.M. Lord and

238

Lady Falaise venture to hope that Lady Elizabeth will accept any hospitality, either for the night or otherwise, which Trefennick can afford.

As the time approached when this visitor was to be expected, Lady Falaise manifested a nervous excitement, which I had not seen in her before.

'You must stay in the room with me, Claire,' she said. We had dropped all formalities by this time.

'I will if Lady Elizabeth does not object,' I said.

'No, you must stay in any case.'

As the time approached when the carriage might be expected, she sent for me into her boudoir.

'Whatever she may say,' she said to me, ' do not leave the room. I cannot bear it unless you are by.'

Very punctually, as it happened, the carriage with the two servants drove up.

We were sitting in that perfect room — Blanche's boudoir — the autumn light flooding it with a roseate glow, when this woman was shown in upon us. She was dressed in a worn, — I fancied at the moment. perhaps uncharitably — affectedly-shabby suit of black. The wan, hunted look in the pale eyes, which had struck me before so sadly, seemed changed now into a passionate excitement, which she made very little effort to control.

'You will not object to my dearest friend, Miss Wand, remaining in the room?' said Lady Falaise.

She paid not the slightest attention either to me or to the words. She sat down for a moment in the seat Lady Falaise indicated to her; but rose immediately, and came up towards the fireplace, standing before Lady Falaise.

'Lady Falaise,' she said, 'I have wanted to see you. I saw you once before, at the room at Minsterley, where you greeted the man whom, I suppose, I must call my husband, with a smile. It is time that you and I met.'

Her manner was so fierce, and her appearance so wild and excited, that I rose in my seat, and stood watching her as I should watch a wild animal about to spring.

'When you came across the room that day,' she went on, 'with your hand held out, you said that you and he were old friends. Liar and perjurer to you — coward, thief, liar, hypocrite to me; and you, Lady Falaise, you, who have chosen to take to yourself a name unsullied for a

thousand years, have dared to say this! You —
false and traitor to your sex! — you, Blanche
Falaise.'

I moved from my place and came nearer to
Blanche, where I stood watching her, for I did
not know what might happen next.

Blanche stood, the carved mantel behind her,
laced from the ceiling with curtains of Indian
silk, that framed a Madonna and child, herself
more like a Madonna than falls to any one's lot
often to see.

Then, as the other paused for a moment, she
came a step forward, her hands held out —

'Oh dear, dear Lady Elizabeth,' she said,
'what can I say to you, to comfort you — you,
whose lot is so much harder than mine? I only
knew him when he was so noble and so good.
Except for that dreadful letter, which was not
himself, I knew nothing else. What can I say
to you, who have passed through so much? I
can say nothing, but to beg of you to remember
how good and noble he was. Oh dear, dear
friend, remember this! You have said well that
we ought to meet. Between us two at least, of
all the women in the world, let there be peace!'

I confess that it seemed to me an impressive
sight, and one which, I might almost say, I

alone, as a woman, had a right to see. These
two, united in so sad and so strange a fellowship, yet in the working out of which, in suffering and in wrong, so different — at enmity even,
as it seemed, between themselves.

I am so impressed with my story, I am so
clear in my admiration of its heroine and of its
end, that I am free from all doubt and appre-
hension that I am 'a traitor to my sex' in
revealing these things. Had I not felt all this
it would have been different, but in that case I
never should have written this story. As it is,
it seems to me that whoever will be shamed by
the narration, it will not be us women. As I
looked at these two, standing upon the hearth, I
seemed to see, as in the crystal brightness of a
clearer air than men breathe, the meaning and
the end of the world-tragedy of woman's life —
a meaning and an end, shadowy, men would call
it — teeming with transcendental life and being,
as it seemed to me.

'Coward and liar as he was,' Lady Elizabeth
went on with no apparent diminution of fierce-
ness; 'I knew nothing of you; I never heard
of you. I thought him everything that a man
ought to be; and you welcome him! you con-
done him! you, Blanche Falaise!'

They stood looking at each other for some
moments as if trying to know more, to understand more.   For a time no one spoke, then she
went on again —

'He deceived me.   He deceived my people.
He took all I had.   He must live in the greatest
style; "it was part of his mission," he said.   He
gambled in shares to make up for his extrava-
gance.   God knows, I spent nothing on myself!
I bought no dresses but the grand ones he made
me buy.   Then he drank, to make up his splen-
did sermons, and to soothe his conscience, as I suppose ; but I daresay you did not know all this.'

'Know it!' said Blanche Falaise, and the
look of pallor and wretchedness in her face
might have moved a cynic, — 'know it!   How
should I know it?   What was your fortune,
Lady Elizabeth Damerle?' she said suddenly,
after a second's pause.

'Fifty thousand pounds.   I inherited from
my great-aunt, the Baroness Rothes.'

'That, at least,' she said, with an almost
startled, radiant look, — 'that, at least, he can
repay.   I have more than that in my hands
which is his by right.   You shall have it whenever you wish.'

Lady Elizabeth gazed at her with wonderment
for a moment.

'Lord Falaise?' she said.

Then for once I saw her smile, the most beautiful thing I ever saw — a smile of supreme confidence, of a certainty amused even at the thought of doubt, and — if you speak of the love of angels — of love.

'I will speak to Lord Falaise,' she said.

The other stood perfectly still, her face becoming gradually more pale. Then she said —

'My God! if I had known this, there would have been no need for him to have gone to jail!'

Blanche caught suddenly at the mantel-shelf behind her, against which she reeled. 'Jail!' she cried.

'Yes,' continued Lady Elizabeth, without regarding her, and with the same desperation of tone and manner that had marked her throughout, — 'yes, the jail. He gave a cheque for two thousand pounds to some one, knowing it to be worthless, and by that he got possession of coupons, or whatever they are called, and gave these to some one else. He had done something of the same kind before, and they were very severe upon him. Still, when he was remanded upon bail, if the two thousand pounds had been paid, it would have been hushed up; but I was not going to ask my people, after all that they had done, and if I had, they would not have given it. I am utterly penniless, as my dress shows. I could not have come down here had not my brother sent me twenty pounds. Still, if I had had two thousand pounds, I would have given it to him — to keep him out of jail!'

'Oh! dear, dear Lady Falaise!'—I was holding her in my arms,—'don't look like that! Speak to me, your own friend, Claire. Speak — oh, speak to me!'

She recovered herself with a sudden effort, and sank down into her chair again. She sat for a few moments looking before her into the fire, then she turned to me with a pitiful, helpless look and gesture which I well understood.

'Lady Elizabeth,' I said, 'we had better leave Lady Falaise for a time. Lord and Lady Falaise are most anxious that you should stay here for the night. I can find you everything you may need; let me try and persuade you.'

We left the room together. As we went out into the gallery above the great staircase, surrounded with family portraits and great cabinets of buhlwork, she said —

'She is more fortunate than I am. It is killing her. Unfortunately it will not kill me. I am made of coarser stuff.'

'I do not think it,' I said. 'It is killing her mind, but not her body. She is more unhappy than you are.'

Lady Elizabeth would not stay at Trefennick. She accepted some slight refreshment, and we sent her back in the carriage to the roadside station, and she got back to London, sometime, I believe; but before she left, Blanche had seen her husband, and the fifty thousand pounds was promised to be settled, at Lord Falaise's especial stipulation, strictly upon Lady Elizabeth Damerle.

I spoke to Lord Falaise once, as I had an opportunity, saying I thought it was wonderfully good of him. He treated it very lightly.

'It is what my father would have done,' he said. 'Besides, the money is not mine; I have enough.'

About a month after this visit we had another surprise. About midday, when the boy had been a second time to the roadside station for letters, Lady Falaise came into the room where I was sitting, with a letter in her hand.

'Read this,' she said, 'and bring it to me when you have done.'

There was something in her manner, in these days, that frightened me. I recalled the words

of that garrulous doctor, and I trembled, as I
watched her leave the room, for I dare not
follow her, at what I ignorantly fancied might
be coming in the future time.   Our faithlessness
is what astonishes me more than anything else.

When she had left the room I read the
letter.

It was dated ——— Jail, and began thus —

My Lord,

Being confined in this place, with nothing but my own
miserable thoughts to occupy me, I feel a strong, an
overpowering impulse to write to you.   The instinct of
confession is one of the most deeply seated, the most
insistent, in the human heart.   It seems, almost, at
times as if the act of confession of sin nullifies sin.   The
Church of Rome, with her usual cleverness, has grasped
this fact up to a certain point, but our own Church, as is
her wont, in a manner of her own, at once more human,
and therefore more touching and pathetic, has also met
this supreme craving and need, for in her case the confession is voluntary and the choice of confessors unlimited; and I, as a churchman, exercise my unfettered
volition, and I choose my own confessor, and I choose
your Lordship.   Why I choose you might appear strange
to some, but it does not seem so to me.   I am convinced
that you are the man whom I have injured more than I
have injured any other man in the world.   This too
might seem strange to some, seeing that it was through
my action that you obtained the woman upon the gaining
of whom your life was set.   But in spite of this I have
no shadow of doubt, and I am perfectly certain that you
have no doubt, that, in the intolerable wrong and injury

I have inflicted upon one whom I dare not name to you, I have done you the most inappeasable wrong that one man can do another. On that memorable evening, when, uncousciously perhaps to all of us, every moment was big with the fate of each of that small company assembled, almost by chance, in a country rectory — on that evening I, in the pride of a vulgar ignorance, regarded *you* with disdain. It will probably be easy for you, in the confidence of an unsullied past, and in the strength of a steadfast present, to look with pity and even with forbearance upon a wretch, of whom it may suffice to say that, as it seems to him, nothing but the annihilation of the race can blot out the memory of the past.

I have said this much that I may explain, in some small degree, what may seem to you to be an extraordinary letter. I will endeavour, in what I write, hereafter to be more plain and precise.

As far as I can look back upon, and understand my past existence, I think that I can trace, not my own fall, for that would not merit a moment's thought, but the evil that I have wrought upon others, to the exuberance of an unrestrained imagination, and from the fact that I regarded Religion as an *end* and not as a *means*. I am more and more convinced that Religion is intended to teach us how to live now, not how to die hereafter.

I imagined numberless evils, which had no likelihood of occurring, and then, because these misfortunes did not happen, I considered myself the peculiar favourite of Heaven. I imagined myself to be especially depicted by Heaven to do certain work, for which I had especial gifts granted me. This last, as far as outward influences extended, and apart from an ineradicable weakness and evil tendency in my own nature, was, so it seems to me now, the immediate cause of my fall.

I write these lines under a feeling of intense mental depression. I have lived for years in the continuous excitement of alcoholic stimulants, and the misery of reaction is more than can be described; yet, in the depths of such misery lies something of a clearer vision if not the promise of an assured hope.

I imagined myself in love — with whom I dare not say — I endowed her with visionary qualities.

I imagined that it was necessary for the work of God that I should attain a position of more commanding influence in the Church and in society; I imagined that I could only obtain this by means of private wealth. When I was told by Dr. Boteraux that it was hopeless, as it seemed then, to expect this from him, I received a great shock. I rallied from it for the time, but I never really recovered from it.

I persuaded myself that I was acting for the best. It is, I am firmly persuaded, from experience both of myself and of others, a certain fact, that anticipated or imagined sin has little or no effect upon the conscience. It is committed sin that stamps the life, and either scorches the conscience into insensibility, or urges it, through the agonies of despair, into repentance. The moment that I had absolutely committed that unpardonable sin, life assumed to me an altogether different guise. Side by side with me, as I walked, there walked another; between me and my wife, as we sat at meat, there sat another, a spectre, impalpable, ghastly, yet wholly real. In the pulpit, at my elbow as I preached, he stood gazing over my shoulder. I preached, it was said, and I myself think, better than ever. It was he, I believe, who suggested the impassioned words; what could gratify incarnate sin more than the taste of the ironic salt of such words, coming from such a wretch as I? I took to drink — God in Heaven, what would not a man take to in such a case as mine?—not common drunkenness, but the constant drinking of the best wine, so that, for months and years together, I do not suppose that I was ever free from the excitement of alcoholic stimulus.

We lived most expensively. We entertained profusely, always with that suave, devil-bated lure, that it was to promote the efficacy of my work for God, and to bring others into His service. 'To lay for souls with Pheasant shooting,' as was said once. I was soon short of cash. I sold out, safe investments, my wife's money. Then I began to speculate upon the Stock Exchange. There is but one end to that. All paths in that dark under world—and there are many—lead to misery and ruin. I became more desperate and more involved as the years rolled on. I was engaged in one or two very shady transactions, through which I contrived to pass by the skin of my teeth, thanks chiefly to that marvellous halo that, even with the most worldly, surrounds a parson. At last I committed the stupidly illegal action that brings me here.

Of course it is impossible for such as I am to hazard a guess whether such a man as you are will show this letter to your wife. If you do, it must surely be a source of constant thankfulness to Lady Falaise that, by the providence of a merciful God, she escaped the unspeakable misfortune of marrying me.

My lord, I can only sign a disgraced and polluted name—

PAUL DAMERLE.

It took me a long time to read this letter. In fact, I read it over three or four times before I began to feel that I had read it at all. Then I tried to arrive at some conclusion with my own mind, as to what I thought of it. Here I was entirely at fault. My mind absolutely refused to answer any question concerning it. Even now, when so many things have happened, I do not seem to have advanced a step. I feel that I must leave it to the reader to decide. What does he think of it?

After I had sat in this state of imbecility for some time, I began to think that I must return the letter to Lady Falaise. I got up and went to her boudoir: she was not there. I went down into the saloon; she was not there. Then I went up into her own rooms and found a maid. — She 'had not the least idea where her ladyship was.' — Then I went downstairs again into the hall, where I met one of the footmen.

'Lord Falaise is out with the boys, I suppose?' I said.

'Yes, Miss Wand. His lordship has been out more than an hour. I should think they will be back soon.'

'Do you know whether her ladyship is in the gardens?' I said.

'No, Miss Wand; I do not know where her ladyship is.'

I put on a hat and cloak, for it was late

in the year, and the day was cold, and went out.

I had some sort of half idea, or rather I hoped that I had. that I should find her in the yew walk, where we had so often been together; but in my heart of hearts, I knew that I had no such hope. That strange and wild letter, whatever it might mean to any of us, what might it mean to her? Something it would most certainly mean. I shuddered to think what it might be, what she might be thinking now of him who had written it, what she might be doing now.

I went out across the wide grass-plot into that drear, ghostly, desolate walk. It stretched itself before me, in the dreariness of its weird length, lined on one side by the bare trees, and on the other by that long, unbroken funereal hedge of darkened yew branches; here and there, where the gardeners had neglected to remove them, hung the dead garlands of the summer wreaths. In the terrible extent of its entire distance there was no one to be seen.

Something. I know not what — for why should I walk along a path, upon which there was evidently no one, to seek for one whom I wished to find — led me on for all this dreary length.

The wailing of the autumn wind; its notes

drawn out and perfected by its passage, and travelling, through miles of woodland, through the withered, moss-grown branches of ancient trees, accompanied me as I went up this grassy walk.

Nothing happened as I went up; only an ever-increasing, overwhelming dread accompanied me step by step.

An overpowering dread, so vague that I could give it no name—would that I had been able to do so!—of what I should find at the end of this path lured me, with a terrible fascination, to go on. I reached the end of the terrace, and nothing had happened; and but for that strange prompting, I should have turned back, for I saw nothing of Lady Falaise anywhere. Nevertheless I went on. At the end of the terrace was a grove of yew trees, which I had often noticed for their solemn depth of shadow, but which I had never thought of piercing through. Now, this irresistible impulse still urging me, I forced my way through the tangled boughs. Underneath was a wide, overarched space, a floor of parched and lifeless ground, thickly covered with the dead debris of the yew branches, that felt soft and still beneath the tread of my feet. I remember that I recalled something that I

had read in some poet of such a wood — so
drear, so lifeless, so arched and shadowed by
death. As I entered, for the light was as clear
beneath these shades as elsewhere, I saw beneath me, in the debris, the faint mark of a
woman's delicate foot. Then I knew what it
was that had led me on.

I followed the shadowy footprints, pointing
with a wavering and uncertain line right
through the wood, and to my surprise — for I
had never penetrated its shades before, nor
known that there was any passage through it —
I came out upon a neglected terrace. stopped
and choked up with the spreading yew
branches. and a flight of stone steps, with stately
balustrades and urns. There were no signs of
footprints here, but I went on down the steps.

There I found myself upon a wide combe or
dingle of the moor, the faded grass of which
stretched out before me on every side, which,
ascending towards the north to a certain eleva-
tion between the higher moorland on either
hand, evidently dipt down again, out of my
sight. in the direction of the sea. Straggling
up this gentle slope. and becoming thicker
towards the top, was a wood of extremely small,
weather-beaten oaks, with lichen-covered boughs,

twisted and contorted into fantastic shapes by the northern gales sweeping up from the sea; and, towards the bottom, where the slope was lost in the level basin of the valley, was a small, dark pool, also shaded by the dwarf oaks. In all this wide solitude, beneath the cloudless winter sky of palest blue, not a living creature was to be seen. The noonday stillness was unbroken by the slightest sound save the almost inaudible whisper of the gentle wind along the grass. I stood perfectly still, stunned suddenly, as it seemed, by a terrible dread.

What if those ghostly, withered trees, standing there for centuries like elfin dwarfs, wicked and malicious, and the dark waters of the pond, knew now another secret, added to the long list of dreary memories — had witnessed, but a few seconds ago, a sadder tragedy than any enacted in the wild, romantic days that were long passed. Should I? had I strength indeed to go on?

Then, as I stood, straining my eyes towards the distant rise, a single figure came out from among the oaks, and came towards me across the level grass. My heart leaped towards it with a sudden, joyful spring and hope, and I moved to meet her very slowly, for it was with difficulty that I could steady myself to walk.

As she came nearer, it seemed to me that her face was altered with a change that would never leave it, and there was a look in her eyes which I had never seen before. I hastened to speak.

'I could not find you in the house and sought for you on the terrace, but I have found what is quite new to me. I never knew before of the path through the yew hedge, or the terrace, or the steps, or of this wild valley.'

I went on speaking, hardly knowing what I said.

'I have only been here once before,' she said in a hushed voice. ·It is a lonely, terrible place. I always told you that I dread the terrace walk itself, and this is more ghostly still. But for God's mercy it would be fatal to me; I will not come again. Let us go back.'

'Yes,' I said, 'here is the letter. Lord Falaise will be back by this time. He is out with the boys.'

V

Lord Falaise took things into his own hands after this, and insisted that we should go abroad. The boys went to a clergyman connected with Eton, in the neighbourhood of Windsor, and were to go to the school after Christmas. We went to the villa on the Riviera, where we stayed into the New Year. Lady Falaise was happier on the Continent than anywhere else, and even attained at times to a certain kind of cheerfulness; but it was evident to me that in spite of this improvement she was greatly changed. and I began to despair. The tone and habit of foreign life, endeared to her by recollections of her girlhood, produced an outward appearance of calm and peace. but underneath. as I knew very well, was an undying misery of regret — an endless struggle which would end only with life itself.

Lord Falaise, as I have said. did not like the Riviera. He especially hated what he called

s   257

'the vulgar rowdyism' of the Battle of Flowers.
He proposed that we should move into South
Austria. I have heard him say that, to his
mind, there was now no country in Europe, saving England, where a gentleman could live at
ease except South Austria. He had been there
before. He was acquainted with the Austrian
nobles. Himself a Norman noble, with as many
quarterings as a Festitic, he was received with
cordiality. So about the middle of February we
left the villa, and made our way through Northern Italy. I believe that our final object was to
reach a certain chateau in the valley of the
Traun, belonging to an Austrian noble, before
the quail-shooting was over; but as we never
reached it, it is not of much consequence what
our finite intention was. The end which was
designed for us we accomplished without let or
fail.

I was constantly with Blanche Falaise—I was
scarcely ever from her side. Before we left the
villa, in the long, lovely afternoons, as we sat by
the open windows, looking out upon the azure
waters, and the brilliant sunlight changed into
the deep colouring of the night, I tried in vain
to rouse her to any real interest in what lay
before her, in any books we read, in any subject

that stirred the world. Still less — when the sun
had sank, and the cold, night air swept across
the gardens, driving even the young and the
happy to take refuge indoors — could I feel that
her heart was there, that she was listening to
what I said, to what I read. Ever her heart
was wandering, I knew, to that man in jail, to
what he suffered and had to bear — always to
that man in jail.

We travelled up by Padua and Traviso, passing Venice, which we saw one evening, from the
railway carriages, rising out of the sea. We
left the line at Udine, and buying carriages, we
drove up into the Carnic Alps, through the Rac-
colano valley and its deep ravines, by Venzone,
with its mediæval walls and its silkworms, and
on to Pontebba, and its foaming torrents and
streams, following the old high road from Italy
to Vienna.

I left behind me, in imagination, the world of
modern fashion and travel, and entered a land
of romance, — a land of mountains and lakes,
of feudal castles upon the craggy summits, of
nobles and serfs, of old-world distinction of rank.
I was not disappointed.

We passed through old towns, with bronze
dragons upon the fountains in their market-

places, and winged eagles upon lofty pillars, and frescoed houses, dim and faint now, but painted, as was said, by Girolamo du Traviso. We walked through quaint arcades running beneath the houses on either side. We went into churches, than which the mind of man or woman conceives nothing so marvellous or wonderful, with Gothic choirs and lancet windows, which were dreams of deepest colour, and mystic signs, and with figures in knightly costume lying upon tombs. Then, ignoring the railways that desecrate this mountain land, we went up through the narrow pass which was, and is, the gate of Italy, on the old Roman road to Vienna that was trodden by Trajan and his legions, and through the old Hercynian forest — that fated wood, full of indescribable terrors, which the Roman legions themselves failed to pierce.

I had expected to see the Alps with a rosy tinge upon the snow, but they faded into the gray clouds of evening, and the next morning, as we drove up the pass, a dense, white mist and vapour settled down upon us, and as we entered into this land of wonders we saw nothing.

All through the long journey over the Italian plain I had watched this long line of shining light, broken here and there with a shade of gray, and now, as we drew near it, it was snatched from my sight.

We drove up the pass in three carriages, steadily hour by hour, in a kind of luminous golden mist and veil which seemed at every moment as though it would lift and reveal to us indescribable things, and yet did not lift, except for an instant here and there, revealing great crags of schist rock, from which the snow had slipped, standing solemn and dark, like guardian sentinels upon either hand.

All around, in this appalling yet luminous mystery, we could hear the rush and fall of mountain torrents, swelled by the melting of the snow, and the thud of the distant avalanches in the higher reaches of the hills.

No possible entrance to a world of romance and wonder, long looked forward to, could have been more impressive than this.

Lord Falaise was, most of the time, alone in the second carriage; I sat with Blanche, for the most part, in silence.

We reached the summit of the pass. still. with the single exception of the momentary vision of the guardian rocks, without sight or knowledge of what was beyond or around us. and began to descend, as we could dimly discern. into the valley of the Drave. Everywhere and always the luminous haze, the enchanted veil, was around us, strange sounds and whisperings seemed to come to us from the distance of hidden rocks.

As we came down into the valley the mist rose, and we found ourselves in an unknown world of beechwoods, over a rushing torrent, and finally drove into a little town where the wizard Paracelsus was said to have been born, with cattle standing at the street-corners, and open shop windows, and women knitting at the doors.

The next morning all was changed. We drove up the valley of the Drave, as I was told the river was called, amid forests of birch and fir, which clothed the bases of the hills, many of which were still covered with snow.

The whole land was full of legends of the valleys and the hills, and we saw, even then, the castles of the old Carinthian chivalry towering above us in the craggy hills against the sky. Nothing seemed impossible in such a land.

The sky was perfectly clear, woods of beech of a brilliant, fresh green colour skirted the road on either side, above them were forests of fir, also of a fresh green, above these banks of moss crept close up against the dazzling snow. The Alps were loftier than any that we had seen before, and above their white summits was a deep, solemn blue sky. We drove slowly and silently up the steep, winding road. The scene was too beautiful to allow of speech.

At the top of the pass, some four thousand feet above the valley, we came upon frozen fields of white and dazzling snow, beyond which rose higher summits, crested with a fairy fretwork of frost tracery pierced with sunlight, and almost transparent against the blue of heaven. I thought at the moment that the mind of man had never conceived anything more lovely than this.

We descended the pass, the snow melting more and more rapidly as we descended, the avalanches in the distant hills and the torrents below us becoming every moment louder and more insistent, and after some time we came upon what seemed a very considerable hotel, where the carriages stopped. Lord Falaise got out of his carriage and went into the house.

The afternoon was inexpressibly beautiful, with that inconstant beauty that belongs to a spring day. There was the sudden hush and stillness that follows when long-continued motion is stayed. We sat in the carriage without a word. A delicious pause and rest — how given and from whence? — seemed to fall upon us suddenly, as we sat side by side. Below us, down the pass, we could discern glimpses of wooded vales, reaching with a soft beauty into the infinite unseen, with faintly drawn, delicate lines and shades, suggestive of a vague yet corresponding effort of thought, of hamlets and villages peeping through the trees, here and there the flashing waves of a lake, the faint smoke of iron forges and charcoal fires. We sat contented and perfectly still.

It has often seemed to me that, at the supreme moments of life, when the fate, not of ourselves alone, which were nothing, but of others, hung in the balance, there has been no effort, no consciousness of necessity even, on our part. Such certainly was it now.

We sat perfectly still — Blanche and I. Above us was a heavenly vision of faint streaks of cloud, drawn and woven and pencilled across the spring azure of the sky. I am certain now, though perhaps I did not know it then, that there was something in this sudden hush and stillness, in this supreme beauty and perfectness that was sent to prepare us for what was to come. 'Cleanse the thoughts of our hearts by the inspiration of Thy Holy Spirit, that we may perfectly love Thee!'

But, the next moment, as I looked, a watery cloud seemed to form itself out of the earth, in the valley, and creep up towards the hills. By little and little it seemed to force itself upon the serene sky above; it fascinated me with an indescribable power and force. I sat looking at this faint gathering cloud, at first no bigger than a man's hand, with an intensity that would have frightened me, had I thought of it at all.

Presently Lord Falaise came out of the hotel.

'It seems a comfortable house,' he said; 'and there is a fall in the valley to the left, which they seem to speak highly of. I think that we had better stay here for the night. You might, perhaps, like to see the fall?' he added, looking at his wife.

'I should like it very much indeed,' she said; 'nothing would please me so much.'

It was always her way, whatever her state; at the slightest suggestion of his, the first thought was, if possible, to please him.

The innkeeper had come out — a Frenchman, with an astonishingly pointed moustache and a white apron.

'The fall is very fine,' he said; 'there is a natural bridge — a great curiosity; my ladies would be very pleased. We have ponies for the ascent. There is also a Calvary, not a Virgin,' he added apologetically, — 'not like the Virgin of Mount Luschari. Ah no! It is a Christ. But it is thought a good deal of here. My ladies may like to see it.'

We got out of the carriage and went into the hotel. It was a good house, very well appointed. The visitors from the watering-places on the lakes, from Velden and Klagenfurt, and from as far as Ischl, came up hither in the summer for the mountain air and the cool breeze. After lunch two ponies were provided, and we went up a parallel valley to the one which we had descended, to the falls.

The afternoon was very hot. It was a very early season, and the melting of the snow was very rapid; as we left the hotel we could see mist rising from the distant valleys beneath us, and, farther off still, over the mountains towards Salzburg, dark masses of cloud were gathering.

'There will be a storm to-morrow, madame,' said one of the men to me; 'but it will be fine here this afternoon.'

We went slowly up the pass. As before, there

were the rushing torrents below us and the winding path — only it was now much narrower — the green beechwood, then the fir reaches, here and there the bare rocky sentinels, and. above all, the snow ranges and peaks.

Suddenly, after ascending for about a mile, we turned a sharp corner of the schist rock, and saw the most beautiful sight that I, for one, shall ever see on this side the grave.

A slight rain-cloud, a forerunner of the coming storm, had followed us up the valley, and a passing shower, delicate and refreshing and quite harmless, passed over us for a second and was gone. To the left lay the vast world of snow mountains, down which we had come a few hours before, with the great masses of bare rock, from which the snow had fallen, standing out stern and cold ; but up towards these snow mountains, and even to their very base, was a bank or meadow of the finest young grass, which, like the warp of the most delicately worked tapestry, was rather suggested than seen, for strewn all over it, in a marvellous tracery of form and colour, were crowded anemones, gentians, cyclamens in groups and families, and scattered lines, and wastes of tinted form ; and, from this broad belt of colour, the snow was visibly melting,

moment after moment, so that the lovely zone
broadened sensibly before the eyes, as by the
motion of a wizard's wand.   To the right, on the
other side of the valley, which was in deep
shadow, masses of wood lay far below us; and
above these, level with ourselves, long lines of
fir forest, and the dark masses of rock, upon
which no sun shone. Before us lay the upward
pilgrim path to the Calvary above, and, higher
still, the broken rocks, falling from the precipitous hillside on either hand, had formed themselves into a marvellous bridge, which crossed
the ravine in front of a fall of water, swollen
now beyond its natural limits, and divided it into
an upper and a lower fall. Across the fallen
rocks a framework of planks and rails led the
way across the ravine to a still narrower path than
the pilgrim path on which we stood, followed
only by the hunters of the izard and the chamois.
At the entrance of this impenetrable path were
carved, as it seemed to us, dim and mystic
traceries upon the rock. A summer sky, though
it was still only early spring, flecked with passing
clouds, faint and delicate as a dream, stretched
itself over our heads; but behind us dark clouds,
rain-laden, were gathering up from the valleys,
and before us over the fall, and the bridge, and

the woods on either hand, and on the mystic carving upon the rocks, and nowhere else, lay a brilliant band and prism of distinct colours, and through these rainbow hues we could see the green tints of the firs and of the beeches, and the dolour of the schist rocks, and the white glamour of the passing snow.

We left the ponies, and, with hushed breathing, as if fearing that the vision would fade at the slightest jarring sound, we followed the pilgrim path.

As we crossed the bridge and approached the opposite side, bewildered by the rush and flash of waters, through which we seemed to pass, and deafened by the ceaseless roar, the dim traceries upon the rock assumed distincter shape. To the right hand, between the rock and the lower fall, was a sort of field, strewn with juniper bushes, and with low mounds of earth and little wooden crosses.

I was walking a little behind Lord and Lady Falaise, and near me was one of the guides who had come up with us from the hotel. I pointed to this strangely strewn field.

'What is this?' I said.

'These are the graves, madame,' he said, 'of unfortunates who have perished in the chamois hunting, in the snows, and,'—he lowered his voice and raised his cap as he went on—'such is the grace of the Saint Calvary, that no grave has ever been torn up, and no corpse mangled by the wolves in this holy ground.'

And when, a minute after, we stood beneath the rock, and gazed up upon this 'Saint Calvary,' we could well fancy that some such legend might be true.

It was carved altogether out of the massive rock; it was not, so at least it seemed to me, a mechanical image or figure, but seemed to be dimly, while perfectly, shaped, and to show itself, as through a veil, as much in a certain vagueness and roughness of handicraft, as in a sacrament or mystery of thought and feeling, as though it were striving and growing into existence, by the gradual and earnest creation of a devout servant of his art, who had sought and found, by prayer and fasting, his ideal in the stony rock. As we neared it, the rainbow hues had faded; yet it seemed to me that there still lingered over it, or it may have been that it was only in my eyes, some delicate colouring, some faint memory of those heavenly tints.

It was a true Calvary of the orthodox type.

It consisted of the three crosses, with their suffering burdens, and a foundation of skull and bones, with two figures standing beneath the crosses, more roughly and carelessly worked — St. John, and the Virgin Mother in a swoon.

There might be something conventional in the treatment of the two thieves — the one writhing with strained and contorted limbs, the other in a rapt attitude of ecstatic gaze; but, if it were so, it seemed only to supply two needed forms of type — the one the restless, unsubdued human nature, the other the saintly, consecrated life. It was evident that the sculptor's thought had been concentrated upon the central figure.

Those momentous hours, laden with the destinies of unimagined existence, were, so at least it seemed to me, drawing to an end. The regal admission into Paradise, the human message to His mother and to His friend, the cry of suffering, even the agony of felt desertion by His Father and His God — all these were over. The last stage of this world-journey, the pilgrimage of the Son of God had arrived. 'It is finished' was bitten into every line, graven by the iron chisel into the dark gray stone.

I have heard that some one says that Wordsworth evoked a sort of soul in matter, and, no doubt, all inanimate beings — plants and flowers and trees — have a certain sort of instinct if not of soul; but here, in the centre of this great Calvary, there was visible a soul in the stolid rock.

For in this figure of a sacrifice that redeemed the world, there was manifested such a sympathy between the genius that grasped the artist's chisel, and the so-called dead rock that lent itself in indescribable shades of light and delicacies of shadow, to the Ideal that lifted a world of pollution and death into one of healthy breezes and of hope, that, as we stood before it, we could no longer wonder that peasants, in their holiday dress, came up the pass to worship with serious and mournful faces, and went back, down the path, singing hymns of joy, for that they were delivered from their sins.

For in this chief figure — this figure that realised the death of God, down-pressed and over-weighted as it was — it was perceptible that the defeat and disaster, however perfect and complete — and no work could give the idea of more perfection and completeness of

suffering and of oppression and of defeat — was
not such as that which ordinary men call by
these names; that even in the moment of
death's triumph the victory was not with
Death; that the defeat and oppression — the
weight of suffering and of grief — were not such
grief and oppression and disaster as befall an
ordinary man; that the death was not such as
awaits a mortal who has finished his course, but
such death as may be imagined of a pilgrim-
God.

Over the whole Calvary, above the rough
grotto-work that fringed the recess which gave
scope for the relief of the figures, like a halo
above the sacred scene, were these words, fas-
tened into the rock in iron letters. moulded, no
doubt, ages since in the iron-works in the
valleys —

VERE LANGUORES NOSTROS IPSE TULET, ET
DOLORES NOSTROS IPSE PORTAVIT.

She stood close by me, clasping my hand.

'Surely He *hath* borne our grief, and carried
our sorrows!' she said.

We returned to the hotel to dinner, and we
slept there, and in the middle of the night came
the storm, at least so it seemed to me. It awoke

me and I lay and listened to it; but it was not the storm itself that I heard, or that kept me from sleep; it was the knowledge of what lay around me — of that wonderful world of mountain and snow and rock. It was the conception of what was happening. at that moment even, in those mountain solitudes. in those vast reaches of snow slopes. of wind-swept hill-meadows and valleys. of what ghastly shapes held wild revel there, what powers of darkness and of storm kept the field.

But in the morning we found that we had been needlessly disturbed. There had been no storm. we were told, only a passing scud and shower; but there were signs of a thunderstorm in the valley. which would probably come up the pass, and, it being so early in the season, might prove alarming. The host admitted this. He would advise the ladies not to venture far from the house.

Lord Falaise, of course. would be likely to go out — in fact, a temptation had been provided for him. He was not satisfied with the horses with which we travelled. The railways which thread the water-courses of the valleys, and even climb some of the lower passes. have very much deteriorated the postal service upon

the roads. Once or twice, in ascending the
passes, we had had to engage extra horses, which
were not to his mind. It was suggested to him
that. at a farm not far down the valley, horses
were to be purchased of a superior kind, bred for
sale in Vienna. 'Milord Anglais,' travelling
with three carriages. was not to be suffered to
pass without toll. The host proposed to send
for the horses to the hotel, but Lord Falaise,
with the eccentricity of his race, preferred to
walk down to the farm. He left the hotel soon
after breakfast, accompanied by his English
groom, who travelled with us.

I sat for some time with Lady Falaise. She
was *distraite.* very *distraite ;* she said something
about prisons and what prisoners had to under-
go. but she did not seem to wish to follow even
this theme. After some time. as she wished to
be alone, I left her. May God forgive me if
what followed was caused by any fault of mine !

To tell the truth. I had a book which I
wished to read — *Histoires D'Hiver.* by the
Vicomte Eugène Melchior de Vogué, which I
had bought in Italy. the first pages of which
only I had found time to read. They had
fascinated me very much.

The perfect French. the most beautiful. I

thought, excepting that of Pascal, which I had
ever read, the tone of distinction with which
the simple stories were treated,—most simple
stories of peasants and servants, after a manner
other from that of some nauseous and vulgar
modern schools which leaves a nasty taste in
the mouth—absorbed and fascinated me more
completely the further I read.

The exquisitely pathetic story of 'Oncle
Fedia,' the quaint Petrouchka and his history,
and the terrible sufferings, which, as a woman,
made my blood run cold within me, of Vavara
Afanasiévna,—all of them, real and commonplace, surely, to the heart's desire, but redeemed
from vulgarity and annoyance because told by a
man of genius who is also a gentleman,—
occupied me for hours. I did not look up until
I had laid down the book.

Lord Falaise came back a little before lunch.
He had not bought the horses. 'They were not
bad,' he said; 'but the people asked an exorbi-
tant price. He was willing to pay an exceptional
price considering the circumstances, but he was
not going to be swindled. They would probably send them up in the afternoon at his own
price.'

The horses indeed came up as he said, but

something else had happened in the meantime.

I had not been aware of it, so absorbed had I
been in my book, but during the morning the
storm-clouds had gathered from the valleys, and
crept up the pass. Rain had begun to fall,
'rather sharply,' Lord Falaise said. He wore a
rough suit with leggings, suitable for the mountains, and did not seem to mind it. 'There was
also thunder in the distance,' he said. The rain
ceased, and an appalling darkness covered the
sky. We were waiting for Lady Falaise to go
in to luncheon.

The next moment a waiter called me out of
the saloon. I went out into the corridor, and
found Lady Falaise's maid, her face white as
death.

'We do not know where her ladyship is,' she
said; 'she is not in her rooms.'

As she spoke, a flash of light, pallid, vivid,
all-pervading, filled the place in which we stood,
drawing us into, and withering us, as it were,
with its ghastly flame, and the next second a
clap of thunder, more terrible, if possible, than
the living fire, fell upon us and upon all the
houses around.

The girl fell to the ground in a heap, burying

her face in her hands. I clasped my hands over my eyes and ears, but otherwise I stood my ground. The next instant another, as livid a flash, burning into our very flesh, followed by as terrific a clap — and then a third — and the storm, driven, as it seemed to me, by a fierce wind, swept up the pass, and left us.

After a minute or two the girl gathered herself up from the ground. She looked at me with her white scared face.

'We have found this,' she said.

She held out a folded letter, which I took. It was addressed —

'The Lord Falaise.'

I went into the saloon to Lord Falaise, the letter in my hand. He looked at me anxiously, as though to see how I had stood the shock.

'They cannot find Blanche anywhere,' I said; 'but they have found this.'

And I gave him the letter, which was not sealed, only folded up.

He took it, and, going into the window, read it through; then he turned it over, and read it again. I sank into one of the great lounges in the saloon, and waited.

He seemed to hesitate for a moment, then he

turned towards me, came back, and handed it to me.

This is what I read —

My Lord —

(Ah me! some one else had begun a letter just like this!)

At last what I have dreaded all these long years, and what I warned you of, is come to pass. He calls me, not by any message or voice of his, but by his suffering and misery, — he calls me, and I must go, if not to him, then somewhere; whither, God knows! Here I cannot stay. The misery and the strain is too intolerable to be borne. When I am gone from you, from this wretched world — oh no, not a wretched world; it is I who am worthless — think of me as of one utterly unworthy, whom you stooped to rescue from the abyss into which she had fallen, gallantly strove to aid and to restore, when aid and rescue were hopeless and all too late, — one who has fallen of her own fault and of none other. I despised all common joys, and all common joys — even the joys of motherhood — have been denied me. Think of me as one upon whom you have lavished such a splendour of love as no woman besides has ever yet received. For twelve long years bearing with what no man besides has ever borne with! What that has been you know even better than I, though I know it all too well; and through all that length of years, not one averted look, never an impatient word. It is impossible but that you must have much to comfort and to console you. It cannot be that, through such as I, a life like yours can be thwarted and ruined. You have the boys. They are wholly yours. No taint of their unhappy mother will ever cling to them. They will grow up to prove themselves what they are — the sons of the noblest and most chivalrous gentleman in the world.   BLANCHE.

I read this letter over twice. as he had done. I turned it over. and examined the creases and the folding. Then I said —

‘Lord Falaise, this letter was not written to-day. nor for many days. I think that I know the day when it was written. Send for all the servants, and ask them where they found this.’

He called the waiter, and told him to send all his servants into the saloon. They came in, looking very scared, as well they might. There were three men — Lord Falaise’s own man, a very superior person. who spoke French and German, a young footman, and the groom. They put the women forward as they came into the room — Lady Falaise’s maid, and a young girl whom, I believe, Blanche had engaged. simply that she might wait upon me.

‘Will you tell me exactly.’ said Lord Falaise, ‘where you found this letter? Was it on her ladyship’s table?’

There was a considerable pause. Then the maid who had come to me said —

‘No, my lord, we found it in my lady’s writing-case.’

'And how dare you.' said Lord Falaise, 'to open her ladyship's writing-case?'

Then the young girl, the under-maid. said —

'We wanted to find out where my lady was.'

'That will do,' said Lord Falaise; and they left the room.

'Lord Falaise,' I said. the moment we were alone; 'believe me, this letter was not written to-day. It was written months ago at Trefennick, in moments of terrible depression and despair. It was written, but her pure spirit and the mercy and love of God being as one, it was never acted upon. only it was not destroyed. I know her. I met her. on the day on which she wrote this letter, in the yew wood, beyond the terrace at Trefennick. and I know where she is now. She is gone up to the Calvary beyond the falls.'

His face turned to a deathly white.

'In this storm?' he said.

I dressed myself as well as I could. We collected together some men who called themselves guides, and some ostlers and people attached to the hotel. and we set off up the pass. There was no rain. only an appalling darkness and cloud everywhere. We could hear the thunder in the distant valleys and hills. but the lightning seemed to have passed away. It seemed to me, or rather I had a strange fancy, that the storm had found in the fastnesses of the mountains some power or storm other than itself, and was engaged in a death-struggle, for we had not gone far before it returned upon us, this time with the wind, for it had gone up the pass against the south wind which had blown steadily for days. Flashes of lightning, followed by thunder-claps, passed over our heads; then it all ceased, and the storm seemed to go down the pass into the valleys from which it had come. But still the dense black cloud lay above our heads as we slowly ascended the pass.

When we came to the turn whence, only the day before, such a vision of loveliness had burst upon my sight, there was nothing of the kind to be seen. The flowers had folded themselves up into the grass, the green tints of the woods seemed to have faded into a sombre hue, and the fall itself seemed hushed and still. Always the dense dark pall of darkness, as of the grave, spread itself over the scene, ever, as it seemed to me, ready to burst in a deluge of rain.

We toiled up the pilgrim path, dreading at every instant what we might see, and crossed the bridge.

As we crossed the bridge—Lord Falaise and I walking first—the black pall suddenly lifted, and seemed to disperse and break itself up into great masses of cloud; and a sudden light from the western sun, brilliant as thought could imagine, spread itself all over the under world, and lighted with a radiant and burning glow all the woods and water and grassy slopes, and the dark rocks, and the distant white summits, and the blue streaks of the glaciers or ice-bands running through the snow. Above us, a pall of blackness and of death; below, a radiance and light breaking, as it were, from the tomb. Behind us rifts of storm-cloud, driven, wreathed and streaked, across a sky of the intensest blue that the eye ever saw; all around us deep calling unto deep, as the avalanches and the rushing torrents spoke from hill to hill; and before us, across the bridge, at the foot of the Calvary, this strange light full upon the divine traceries upon the stony rock, lay Lady Falaise, one small black spot upon her shoulder, where the lightning had struck.

It is the good that suffer here. ‘You have only to be bad enough,’ says the cynic, ‘and you may live on *pâté de foie gras* and champagne to the end of your days; and the uncomplaining stillness of broken hearts, of wives, and mothers, and sisters is unheeded, as it seems to you, by the God of Sabaoth.' It is a truth as old as time, and the pagans knew it as well as we: 'In very faithfulness hast Thou afflicted me;' 'Whom the gods love they slay.' And they tell us, with their patient voices and their pleading eyes, that suffering, with the people of God, is to be preferred to *pâté de foie gras* with the servants of sin, and that they who have tasted of this bitter but invigorating cup, scarcely care to pray that it be taken away.

Something more than three weeks afterwards, as we rested in Paris on our way home, I received a letter from Lady Elizabeth Damerle, which I insert here —

I have just seen in the papers the death of Lady Falaise in the Austrian Alps, and I can scarcely breathe for awe. I will tell you what has happened to me.

As near as I can calculate, the day on which she died was the day on which my husband's term of imprisonment came to an end. I had taken some rooms in Bloomsbury, and I had sent word to the governor of the jail where I was. I do not know why I had done this, for my heart was as hard as flint against my husband, and I said that I wished that I might never see him again. Nevertheless, it is a fact that I had done it.

I was sitting in my room — the shabby room of a London lodging, perhaps you may know what that is — on the very afternoon, as I believe, on which Lady Falaise died, and I was wondering whether my husband would dare to come to me. He did not know — at least I had no reason to suppose that he knew — that I had any money. I thought that probably he would not come. I hoped that he would not come. I set my face against him like a flint, and yet I could not but remember that Lady Falaise had given me back all that money, and that she had said that it was his. I suppose that it was for that reason that I had sent the governor word where I was.

It was a dull, cold, spring day in London, a north-east wind biting through the streets. Across the street, from my windows, the opposite houses pressed upon me, dull and blackened by the smoke.

Suddenly, as it seemed to me for no reason — for I had not begun to think of her before — I began to think of Lady Falaise. I thought of that afternoon when I had gone down to Trefennick, and how I had seen her and you. I remembered how she had looked, standing against the fireplace, when she had pleaded for him. I remembered her look. I do not know that women are particularly taken by the looks of other women — at any rate, I do not think that I am; but I remembered, with a sort of strange admiration, how she had looked when she had pleaded for him.

There seemed a wonderful stillness in the air. The uproar of the London streets, the jargon of discordant sounds, instead of jarring upon the ear, seemed lulled into a sort of harmony and hush of sound — a hush that spoke through stillness with a power greater than that of speech. I remembered particularly that this hush and stillness struck me. I think that I associated it in some way with

Lady Falaise. I have read that 'there is a supreme Art that rules the world, and that can subdue all things, even the most discordant, to itself.' I believe it now.

I fell into a kind of dream or trance — I say trance, because I do not think that I was asleep in the common sense of the word. In my trance, or dream, or sleep, I thought that I was wandering under a dense pall or cloud as of an endless vault or grave. The intense darkness settled down upon me with a weight and oppression indescribable in words, and my spirit was borne down with a terror and a trouble which I could not explain, until it suddenly flashed upon me that I was lost in the catacombs of Rome.

No words that I can invent can describe what I suffered, — the horror of a lost clue, the blankness of darkness for ever — during the hours of a bright Italian afternoon which I spent with a gay company in those ghastly vaults and shades. Now, strange as it may seem, when I realised where I was, I felt an instantaneous relief.

In my trance or dream, with a lightened heart, I wandered on. The gloom and the darkness seemed terrible no more. Suddenly, so suddenly that it was moments before I was conscious of it, I saw a light. No language of mine can describe this light, so different was it from anything of earth; and, in the centre of this light — and now I knew more surely that I was in the catecombs — was a shepherd with a lamb. It was carved only, as it seemed to me — so flat and faint it was — upon the wall, over an altar, which itself was traced only upon the wall. The unspeakable light, that no man can approach unto, became clearer and more clear, and in the midst of it, before the altar, stood Lady Falaise; and it seemed to me, during the moment that I saw the vision, that words were spoken to her which rang in my ears, as, when one

wakes from a dream, something of the mystery seems to
linger for a few seconds upon the sense —

'Thou hast tried to offer a sacrifice which it was not
for thee to offer, and to bear a punishment which was not
thine to suffer or to bear. Nevertheless, the sacrifice
which thou hadst to offer is accepted, and the punishment which was thine thou hast fully borne. Thy prayer
is heard. His sins, which are many, are forgiven him.
He is turned, and shall be saved.'

And I awoke from my dream, or trance, or sleep,
and there was a noise at the door, and my husband
came in.

He was very pale and worn; but there was a look in
his face which I had never seen there before. He sank
upon his knees on the threshold of the room; and I went
to him, and I raised him up, and I kissed him on the
forehead; and I said to him —

'My husband, it is meet that we should forgive each
other, needing so much forgiveness for ourselves;' and
we knelt down together in prayer to God.

A month ago I was at Trefennick, and sat
with my aunt in the nave, in the same seat from
which I had first seen Lady Falaise. She has a
tomb to herself in the chancel. with her titles,
and the quarterings of the Falaise arms above.
and a space below for her husband's name; but
above the seat where Lord Falaise — he is very
white. though he is not yet fifty years of age —
sits alone (the boys are at Eton) is an escutcheon

of marble with black letters upon the white shield —

IN MEMORY OF
BLANCHE
VISCOUNTESS FALAISE.

I had thought to stop here; but, in turning over these leaves, I came upon this passage, which I transcribed from her diary, written in the first glow of her young faith and gratitude and hope —

'What can I do to deserve such gracious treatment? How can I possibly live so as not to discredit it? — some fruitful harvest, some great future — it seems impossible, nay, faithless, to doubt — must be intended where such blessing is given now.'

Something, I know not what, tells me that no words are so befitting to end with as are these.

THE END

Typography by J. S. Cushing & Co., Boston, U.S.A.

Presswork by Berwick & Smith, Boston, U.S.A.

MACMILLAN'S DOLLAR NOVELS.

Macmillan & Co. beg to announce that they will publish during the Autumn a Series of Copyright Novels, by well-known authors, at the uniform price of one dollar per volume. The following volumes are in active preparation : —

LIFE'S HANDICAP. Stories of Mine Own People. By RUDYARD KIPLING. (The greater part of these stories are now first published.) *Ready.*

THE WITCH OF PRAGUE. A Fantastic Tale. By F. MARION CRAWFORD. With numerous illustrations. *Ready.*

A SYDNEY SIDE SAXON. By ROLF BOLDREWOOD, author of "A Colonial Reformer," "Robbery Under Arms." *Ready.*

TIM : A Story of School Life. By a New Writer. *Ready.*

CECILIA DE NOËL. By the author of "Mademoiselle Ixe." *Ready Oct. 9.*

BLANCHE, LADY FALAISE. By J. H. SHORTHOUSE, author of "John Inglesant." *Ready Oct. 16.*

THE BURNING OF ROME. A Story of the Days of Nero. By the Rev. Prof. A. T. CHURCH. *In the Press.*

THAT STICK. By CHARLOTTE M. YONGE, author of "The Heir of Redclyffe." *In the Press.*

NEVERMORE. By ROLF BOLDREWOOD, author of "Robbery under Arms," etc.

DAVID. By Mrs. HUMPHRY WARD, author of "Robert Elsmere," "Amiel's Journal," etc.

THE RAILWAY MAN AND HIS CHILDREN. By Mrs. OLIPHANT.

MACMILLAN & CO.,

112 FOURTH AVENUE, NEW YORK.

WORKS BY J. H. SHORTHOUSE.

12MO, CLOTH, $1.00 EACH.

—

BLANCHE, LADY FALAISE.

Ready Oct. 16th.

JOHN INGLESANT.

A ROMANCE.

Will always attract men who think, the studious few, the "elect" of literature. Its sale has been constant, and here in America it has passed through six editions in as many years. . . . The naturalness of the story is its abounding charm. . . . Merits the high praise of Mr. Gladstone that, of its kind, "it is the greatest work since 'Romola.'"—A. F. HUNTER, in *Boston Daily Advertiser.*

May be safely called the most remarkable historical romance which has appeared since "Hypatia." . . . Unquestionably one of the finest historical studies in our language. — *Christian Union.*

SIR PERCIVAL.

A STORY OF THE PAST AND OF THE PRESENT.

The story of Sir Percival and Constance is very touching and beautiful, and it is set with alluring pictures of quiet life in an aristocratic country-house, among gentle people. — *New York Tribune.*

THE LITTLE SCHOOL-MASTER MARK.

A SPIRITUAL ROMANCE.

Of this remarkable story, if it may be called a story, we can only say that it will bear reading many times, and that its profound spiritual meaning will come out more and more every time it is read. — *Mail and Express.*

A TEACHER OF THE VIOLIN,

AND OTHER TALES.

There is a nobility and purity of thought, a delicacy of touch, and a spiritual insight which have endeared the work of this author to a large class of readers, and his latest book is one to more than satisfy expectation. — *Boston Courier.*

THE COUNTESS EVE.

It is, after "John Inglesant," the most impressive of the author's works. . . . The story is told with unfailing delicacy and unflagging power. Its effect is spiritualizing. — *Chicago Tribune.*

—◆—

MACMILLAN & CO.,

112 FOURTH AVENUE, NEW YORK.

WORKS BY MRS. HUMPHRY WARD.

DAVID.

12mo, cloth, $1.00. *Shortly.*

ROBERT ELSMERE.

12mo, cloth, $1.00 ; Library Edition, 2 vols., $3.00.

The book is a drama in which every page is palpitating with intense and real life. It is a realistic novel in the highest sense of the word. — *The Whitehall Review.*

Comparable in sheer intellectual power to the best works of George Eliot. . . . Unquestionably one of the most notable works of fiction that has been produced for years. — *The Scotsman.*

MR. GLADSTONE writes of this Novel in the '' Nineteenth Century.''

The strength of the book seems to lie in an extraordinary wealth of diction, never separated from thought; in a close and searching faculty of social observation; in generous appreciation of what is morally good, impartially exhibited in all directions; above all, in the sense of omission with which the writer is evidently possessed, and in the earnestness and persistency of purpose with which through every page and line it is pursued. The book is eminently an offspring of the time, and will probably make a deep, or at least a very sensible impression; not, however, among mere novel-readers, but among those who share, in whatever sense, the deeper thought of the period.

AMIEL'S JOURNAL.

THE JOURNAL INTIME OF HENRI-FREDERIC AMIEL.

TRANSLATED, WITH AN INTRODUCTION AND NOTES. WITH A PORTRAIT.

New and Cheaper Edition. 12mo, $1.75.

A wealth of thought and a power of expression which would make the fortune of a dozen less able works. — *Churchman.*

A work of wonderful beauty, depth, and charm. . . . Will stand beside such confessions as St. Augustine's and Pascal's. . . . It is a book to converse with again and again: fit to stand among the choicest volumes that we esteem as friends of our souls. — *Christian Register.*

MISS BRETHERTON.

12mo, cloth (uniform with " Robert Elsmere "), $1.25.

It shows decided character and very considerable originality. . . . It is full of earnest womanly sympathy with the ambitions of a beautiful girl placed in false and difficult positions by good fortune, which may possibly turn to misfortune. . . . We are impressed throughout by the refinement and the evidence of culture which underlie all the book, though they are seldom or never obtruded. — *London Times.*

MILLY AND OLLY;

OR, A HOLIDAY AMONG THE MOUNTAINS.

16mo, $1.00.

ILLUSTRATED BY MRS. ALMA-TADEMA.

The present season will scarcely see a more charming addition to children's literature than this of Mrs. Ward's. Her book has seemed to us all that a Christmas gift for a child should be. — *Academy.*

MACMILLAN & CO.,

112 FOURTH AVENUE, NEW YORK.

WORKS BY RUDYARD KIPLING.

LIFE'S HANDICAP.

STORIES OF MINE OWN PEOPLE.

12mo, cloth, $1.00.

In this volume the following stories are published for the first time :

THE FINANCES OF THE GODS.
THE LANG MEN O' LARUT.
REINGELDER AND THE GERMAN FLAG.
THE WANDERING JEW.
THROUGH THE FIRE.
THE AMIR'S HOMILY.
JEWS IN SHUSHAN.
THE LIMITATIONS OF PAMBE SERANG.
LITTLE TOBRAH.
BUBBLING WELL ROAD.
THE CITY OF DREADFUL NIGHT.
GEORGIE PORGIE.
NABOTH.
THE DREAM OF DUNCAN PARRENNESS.

No volume of his yet published gives a better illustration of his genius, and of the weird charm which have given his stories such deserved popularity. — *Boston Daily Traveller.*

Some of Mr. Kipling's best work is in this volume. Mr. Kipling is a literary artist of the first rank, and everything in the way of short stories he has written thus far has proved itself to be well worth the reading. — *Boston Beacon.*

PLAIN TALES FROM THE HILLS.

12mo, cloth, $1.50.

Every one knows that it is not easy to write good short stories. Mr. Kipling has changed all that. Here are forty of them, averaging less than eight pages apiece; there is not a dull one in the lot. Some are tragedy, some broad comedy, some tolerably sharp satire. The time has passed to ignore or undervalue Mr. Kipling. He has won his spurs and taken his prominent place in the arena. This, as the legitimate edition, should be preferred to the pirated ones by all such as care for honesty in letters. — *Churchman.*

THE LIGHT THAT FAILED.

12mo, $1.50.

"The Light that Failed" is an organic whole — a book with a backbone — and stands out boldly among the nerveless, placid, invertebrate things called novels that enjoy an expensive but ephemeral existence in the circulating libraries. — *Athenæum.*

MACMILLAN & CO.,

112 FOURTH AVENUE, NEW YORK.

F. MARION CRAWFORD'S NOVELS.

12MO. BOUND IN CLOTH.

THE WITCH OF PRAGUE.

A FANTASTIC TALE.

With numerous Illustrations by W. J. HENNESSY.

Price, $1.00.

"The Witch of Prague" is so remarkable a book as to be certain of as wide a popularity as any of its predecessors. The keenest interest for most readers will lie in its demonstration of the latest revelations of hypnotic science. . . . But "The Witch of Prague" is not merely a striking exposition of the far-reaching possibilities of a new science; it is a romance of singular daring and power. — *London Academy.*

KHALED:

A TALE OF ARABIA.

Price, $1.25.

The story is powerful; it is pervaded by fine poetic feeling, is picturesque to a remarkable degree, and the local color is extraordinary in its force and truth. Of the many admirable contributions to the literature of fiction that Mr. Crawford has made, this book is, on the whole, the most artistic in construction and finish, and the thorough artist is apparent at every stage of the story. His plot is intensely dramatic, but he has never permitted it to sway him to the extent of slighting any of the more minute details under the impulse of merely telling what he has to tell. He holds his theme firmly in hand and controls instead of being controlled by it. The characters have been drawn with the greatest care and stand out in bold relief and fine contrast. The atmosphere of the East is in every page, in every utterance. — *Boston Saturday Evening Gazette.*

Throughout the fascinating story runs the subtlest analysis, suggested rather than elaborately worked out, of human passion and motive, the building out and development of the character of the woman who becomes the hero's wife and whose love he finally wins being an especially acute and highly-finished example of the story-teller's art. . . . That it is beautifully written and holds the interest of the reader, fanciful as it all is, to the very end, none who know the depth and artistic finish of Mr. Crawford's work need be told. — *The Chicago Times.*

MACMILLAN & CO.,

112 FOURTH AVENUE, NEW YORK.

F. MARION CRAWFORD'S NOVELS.

12MO. BOUND IN CLOTH.

A CIGARETTE-MAKER'S ROMANCE.
Price, $1.25.

It is a touching romance, filled with scenes of great dramatic power. — *Boston Commercial Bulletin.*

It is full of life and movement, and is one of the best of Mr. Crawford's books. — *Boston Saturday Evening Gazette.*

The interest is unflagging throughout. Never has Mr. Crawford done more brilliant realistic work than here. But his realism is only the case and cover for those intense feelings which, placed under no matter what humble conditions, produce the most dramatic and the most tragic situations. . . . This is a secret of genius, to take the most coarse and common material, the meanest surroundings, the most sordid material prospects, and out of the vehement passions which sometimes dominate all human beings to build up with these poor elements scenes and passages, the dramatic and emotional power of which at once enforce attention and awaken the profoundest interest. *New York Tribune.*

MR. ISAACS.
A Tale of Modern India.   Price, $1.50.

If considered only as a semi-love story it is exceptionally fascinating, but when judged as a literary effort it is truly great. — *Home Journal.*

Under an unpretentious title we have here the most brilliant novel, or rather romance, that has been given to the world for a very long time. — *The American.*

No story of human experience that we have met with since "John Inglesant" has such an effect of transporting the reader into regions differing from his own. "Mr. Isaacs" is the best novel that has ever laid its scenes in our Indian dominions. — *The Daily News.*

A work of unusual ability. . . . It fully deserves the notice it is sure to attract. — *The Athenæum.*

A story of remarkable freshness and promise, displaying exceptional gifts of imagination. — *The Academy.*

DR. CLAUDIUS.
A True Story.   Price, $1.50.

An interesting and attractive story, and in some directions a positive advance upon "Mr. Isaacs." — *New York Tribune.*

"Dr. Claudius" is surprisingly good, coming after a story of so much merit as "Mr. Isaacs." The hero is a magnificent specimen of humanity, and sympathetic readers will be fascinated by his chivalrous wooing of the beautiful American countess. — *Boston Traveller.*

MACMILLAN & CO.,
112 FOURTH AVENUE, NEW YORK.

F. MARION CRAWFORD'S NOVELS.

12MO. BOUND IN CLOTH.

ZOROASTER.
Price, $1.50.

The novel opens with a magnificent description of the march of the Babylonian court to Belshazzar's feast, with the sudden and awful ending of the latter by the marvelous writing on the wall which Daniel is called to interpret. From that point the story moves on in a series of grand and dramatic scenes and incidents which will not fail to hold the reader fascinated and spell-bound to the end. — *Christian at Work.*

The field of Mr. Crawford's imagination appears to be unbounded. . . . In "Zoroaster" Mr. Crawford's winged fancy ventures a daring flight. . . . Yet "Zoroaster" is a novel rather than a drama. It is a drama in the force of its situations and in the poetry and dignity of its language, but its men and women are not men and women of a play. By the naturalness of their conversation and behavior they seem to live and lay hold of our human sympathy more than the same characters on a stage could possibly do. — *The Times.*

A TALE OF A LONELY PARISH.
Price, $1.50.

It is a pleasure to have anything so perfect of its kind as this brief and vivid story. . . . It is doubly a success, being full of human sympathy, as well as thoroughly artistic in its nice balancing of the unusual with the commonplace, the clever juxtaposition of innocence and guilt, comedy and tragedy, simplicity and intrigue. — *Critic.*

SARACINESCA.
Price, $1.50.

His highest achievement, as yet, in the realms of fiction. The work has two distinct merits, either of which would serve to make it great, — that of telling a perfect story in a perfect way, and of giving a graphic picture of Roman society in the last days of the Pope's temporal power. . . . The story is exquisitely told. — *Boston Traveller.*

One of the most engrossing novels we have ever read. — *Boston Times.*

MARZIO'S CRUCIFIX.
Price, $1.50.

Now this is brought out in this little story with the firmness of touch, a power and skill which belong to the first rank in art. . . . We take the liberty of saying that this work belongs to the highest department of character painting in words. — *Churchman.*

"Marzio's Crucifix" is another of those tales of modern Rome which show the author so much at his ease. A subtle compound of artistic feeling, avarice, malice, and criminal frenzy is this carver of silver chalices and crucifixes. — *The Times.*

MACMILLAN & CO.,

112 FOURTH AVENUE, NEW YORK.

F. MARION CRAWFORD'S NOVELS.

12MO. BOUND IN CLOTH.

WITH THE IMMORTALS.

Price, $2.00.

Altogether an admirable piece of art worked in the spirit of a thorough artist. Every reader of cultivated tastes will find it a book prolific in entertainment of the most refined description, and to all such we commend it heartily. — *Boston Saturday Evening Gazette.*

GREIFENSTEIN.

Price, $1.50.

"Greifenstein" is a remarkable novel, and while it illustrates once more the author's unusual versatility, it also shows that he has not been tempted into careless writing by the vogue of his earlier books. . . . There is nothing weak or small or frivolous in the story. The author deals with tremendous passions working at the height of their energy. His characters are stern, rugged, determined men and women, governed by powerful prejudices and iron conventions, types of a military people, in whom the sense of duty has been cultivated until it dominates all other motives, and in whom the principle of "noblesse oblige" is so far as the aristocratic class is concerned, the fundamental rule of conduct. What such people may be capable of is startlingly shown. — *New York Tribune.*

SANT' ILARIO.

A SEQUEL TO "SARACINESCA."

Price, $1.50.

The author shows steady and constant improvement in his art. "Sant' Ilario" is a continuation of the chronicles of the Saracinesca family. . . . A singularly powerful and beautiful story. . . . Admirably developed, with a naturalness beyond praise. . . . It must rank with "Greifenstein" as the best work the author has produced. It fulfils every requirement of artistic fiction. It brings out what is most impressive in human action, without owing any of its effectiveness to sensationalism or artifice. It is natural, fluent in evolution, accordant with experience, graphic in description, penetrating in analysis, and absorbing in interest. — *New York Tribune.*

MACMILLAN & CO.,

112 FOURTH AVENUE, NEW YORK

9 783337 089283